THE BARBARA CARTLAND ETERNAL COLLECTION

The Barbara Cartland Eternal Collection is the unique opportunity to collect all five hundred of the timeless beautiful romantic novels written by the world's most celebrated and enduring romantic author.

Named the Eternal Collection because Barbara's inspiring stories of pure love, just the same as love itself, the books will be published on the internet at the rate of four titles per month until all five hundred are available.

The Eternal Collection, classic pure romance available worldwide for all time .

I0620843

NEVER LOSE LOVE

Barbara Cartland

Barbara Cartland Ebooks Ltd

This edition © 2018

Copyright Cartland Promotions 1994

ISBNs

9781788671491   EPUB

9781788671507   PAPERBACK

Book design by M-Y Books
m-ybooks.co.uk

THE LATE DAME BARBARA CARTLAND

Barbara Cartland, who sadly died in May 2000 at the grand age of ninety eight, remains one of the world's most famous romantic novelists. With worldwide sales of over one billion, her outstanding 723 books have been translated into thirty six different languages, to be enjoyed by readers of romance globally.

Writing her first book 'Jigsaw' at the age of 21, Barbara became an immediate bestseller. Building upon this initial success, she wrote continuously throughout her life, producing bestsellers for an astonishing 76 years. In addition to Barbara Cartland's legion of fans in the UK and across Europe, her books have always been immensely popular in the USA. In 1976 she achieved the unprecedented feat of having books at numbers 1 & 2 in the prestigious B. Dalton Bookseller bestsellers list.

Although she is often referred to as the 'Queen of Romance', Barbara Cartland also wrote several historical biographies, six autobiographies and numerous theatrical plays as well as books on life, love, health and cookery. Becoming one of Britain's most popular media personalities and dressed in her trademark pink, Barbara spoke on radio and television about social and political issues, as well as making many public appearances.

In 1991 she became a Dame of the Order of the British Empire for her contribution to literature and her work for humanitarian and charitable causes.

Known for her glamour, style, and vitality Barbara Cartland became a legend in her own lifetime. Best remembered for her wonderful romantic novels and loved by millions of readers worldwide, her books remain treasured for their heroic heroes, plucky heroines and traditional values. But above all, it was Barbara Cartland's overriding belief in the positive power of love to help, heal and improve the quality of life for everyone that made her truly unique.

AUTHOR'S NOTE

The Parish Church of St. George, Hanover Square was built in 1716 on land given by General William Stuart, one of the first residents of Hanover Square.

The architect of St. George's was John James and it is a beautifully simple building in the Palladian tradition of Wren.

It was one of the fifty Churches planned by Parliament in the reign of Queen Anne to replace the many London Churches destroyed during the Great Fire.

But the Church was not often used for burials and the Parish Burying Ground further West between Mount Street and South Street was used until it filled up.

The Grosvenor Chapel, which was on one side of it, Sir Richard Grosvenor built in 1730.

It is today one of the most charming relics of eighteenth century Mayfair.

Brick built with a spire in plain Colonial style, it was copied in countless American towns and hamlets.

Among those buried deep in their mysteriously blocked off vaults are known to be Lady Mary Stuart Wellesley Montague, John Wilkes the populist

Reformer and The Earl and Countess of Mornington, who were the parents of the Duke of Wellington.

CHAPTER ONE
1879

"Mama – *Mama!*"

Josina ran straight to her mother's bed and bent over her.

"I am here, Mama," she said. "What has happened? What is the matter?"

Lady Margaret Marsh looked slowly up at her daughter.

'Y-you are – here – darling," she murmured in a hesitating voice.

Josina sat down on the side of the bed.

"But you are ill, Mama!" she exclaimed. "Why did you not send for me sooner?"

"I – wanted to see you – darling," Lady Margaret mumbled, "And now – you have come that is all – that matters."

Josina looked at her mother with worried eyes.

Lady Margaret had, since her husband's death, become extremely thin and pale and it seemed now to Josina as if she had shrunk into something much smaller and more fragile than she remembered.

Her mother was silent and she rose from the bed.

Taking off her hat she put it down on a chair.

She was wearing the plain dress that was almost a uniform at the Convent School in Florence where she had been living for the last two years.

When the Mother Superior had sent for her, she had wondered what had happened.

"I have had a letter from your mother, Josina," the Mother Superior said quietly. "She wants you to go to her at once."

"At once?" Josina replied. "What is wrong?"

"I don't know," the Mother Superior replied, "but I have arranged for Sister Benedict to take you in an hour's time."

She did not seem to want to answer any more questions.

So Josina hurried away to her room to pack her clothes.

She had been leaving the Convent anyway at the end of the term, but it was really surprising that her mother had sent for her three weeks earlier.

She could not imagine what could be wrong and, all the time that she was travelling with Sister Benedict in the slow train that ran between Florence and the small town of Pavia where her mother was living, she was turning it over and over in her mind.

In fact she never stopped until she entered the house and was told by the Italian maid that Lady Margaret was in her bedroom and that she was ill.

Now Josina knew perceptively that her mother was not only ill but very sick indeed.

She felt as if the knowledge was like a cold hand squeezing her heart.

She wondered frantically what she could do.

At the same time she was sensible enough to know that she must be calm and quiet and listen respectfully to what her mother had to say to her.

The windows were open in her bedroom and there was a cool breeze blowing out the curtains and the frill round the bed cover.

Forcing herself to walk slowly, Josina went up to the bed.

Her mother's hand was resting on the sheet and, when she touched it, she found that it was very cold.

It was in fact so cold that she stiffened and her eyes were very apprehensive as she said softly,

"I am here – Mama darling."

Lady Margaret opened her eyes.

"There are – some drops on the – table,' she whispered, "that the – doctor has left. Please put – three of them on – my tongue."

Her voice was very low and the words disjointed and without speaking Josina did as she was told.

The little black bottle looked, Josina thought, decidedly sinister.

She then pulled out the stopper and very gently squeezed three drops into her mother's mouth.

Lady Margaret drew a deep breath.

Almost a minute must have passed before she opened her eyes again saying, and her voice was stronger,

"I-I feel – better. Now listen to – me, darling."

"I am listening, Mama," Josina responded, "I cannot think why you have not sent for me before. Of course I would have come at once."

"I – know that," Lady Margaret said, "but – I wanted you to – finish your – education, but now – there is no time."

"No time?" Josina repeated beneath her breath.

Lady Margaret took a deep breath and then she said,

"I am going to – die, my precious little – daughter and there is nothing the – doctors can do – therefore we have to be – very sensible and face – the future for you."

Josina made a little sound that was like the cry of a child.

She bent forward and kissed her mother's cheek.

"I love you – I love you, Mama," she exclaimed. "How can you – leave me – when I need you so much?"

"That is – what worries me," Lady Margaret replied, "but you know – darling – that I shall be with – Papa – and that is what I want – above all else."

Josina bit back the words that came to her lips because she knew that they were selfish.

She had known, ever since her father had died fighting a stupid and unnecessary duel, that her mother found it impossible to live without him.

She had never been strong and, from the moment she became a widow and alone, she seemed to wither more each day, so that it was frightening to watch.

She had sent Josina back to the Convent School telling her not to worry.

But Josina reflected now that she had really known when the summons had come to return home that this was the reason.

She did not speak, but merely raised her mother's hand to her lips and kissed it gently.

"Now – listen to me – very carefully," Lady Margaret insisted in a weakening voice, "because – I have everything – planned and you have to – promise me that you will – do exactly as I say."

"Of course I will, Mama," Josina replied, "but what – will I do – without you?"

Her voice broke on the last words.

Then, because she knew that to make a scene would upset her mother, she forced herself to be controlled.

"I-I have been – thinking," Lady Margaret continued, "of – what you can do, darling – and the answer is – quite clear in my – mind. You must – go to my old home and I have – written a letter asking the – new Duke of Nevondale to – look after you."

Josina stared at her mother wide-eyed.

"The Duke?" she queried, "but, Mama, he will refuse! None of your family have spoken or written to you since you ran away with – Papa."

"I – realise that, my darling," Lady Margaret said, "but you – know when my father – died he had no – heir as both my brothers were – killed when they were in the Army. The relative who will – have inherited the title – is a very distant cousin and I have never – even seen him."

"Then – why," Josina asked, "should he take any interest in me?"

"Because – my dear – he is Head of the Family and as the Head – he has a responsibility for every – member of the – Nevons, whoever and – wherever they are."

"But – Mama – " Josina began.

Lady Margaret made a very slight movement and then said quietly,

"Let – me – talk."

Josina put her cheek against her mother's hand, which she was still holding in hers.

"I am listening," she nodded.

"As soon as – I die," Lady Margaret said, "and the – doctor has told me that he will – make all the arrangements for my – funeral, you are to go to – England."

Again she drew a deep breath before she went on,

"Alas, we cannot – afford a – Courier, but I have put by what I think is – enough for your First – Class ticket."

Josina was about to protest that it seemed an unnecessary extravagance, but before she could do so, Lady Margaret went on,

"I hate the idea of you – travelling alone – and it worries me. You must therefore – darling, do exactly as I – tell you to do – and that is to wear – my Wedding ring."

Josina stared at her mother in bewilderment, but Lady Margaret carried on determinedly,

"You will – travel as 'Mrs. Marsh' – and you will – wear my black gown and the widow's hat that I wore at your – father's funeral."

There was a pause and then Josina asked her,

"I think I understand, Mama. You think it would be wrong for me to travel alone – as a young girl."

"Of course – it would be — wrong," Lady Margaret agreed, "and strange men might – take advantage of the fact – but I feel – looking like a widow – you will be left alone – and it would be wise, my precious, if you pulled the – veil over your pretty face."

She closed her eyes as if what she had said had been a great effort and after a few minutes Josina declared,

"I will do exactly as you say, Mama, and now I think – I understand."

"You will find – the money in my – purse," Lady Margaret said with difficulty, "and – you will have to – spend it – very carefully because – we have nothing – nothing else left."

Josina looked at her mother in consternation.

"N-nothing, Mama?"

"Nothing!" Lady Margaret repeated. "I have – had to – pay the doctor and I have also given – him the money for my coffin. You may be able to get – a little money for what is – left. But what is important is that you should – leave here – immediately I am – dead."

With a struggle she made her voice firmer and louder as she persisted,

"Promise me – *promise me* – on everything you hold sacred – that you will – go to the Duke."

"Of course I will – if that is what you want me to do," Josina agreed, "but supposing, Mama, just supposing because the family were so angry with you that he then – sends me away?"

"He will – not do that," Lady Margaret replied positively. "It would be – against the family's pride to let you – starve in the – gutter and perhaps, just perhaps, one of the other members of the family – will have forgiven me – after all these years."

Josina could not help thinking that this was unlikely.

She had heard the story so often of how her mother, who was the daughter of the fourth Duke of Nevondale, had learned that a marriage had been arranged for her with Prince Frederick of Lucenhoff.

Lucenhoff was a small Principality on the border between Germany and Austria.

It was a union that had pleased Queen Victoria and she had given a dinner party for the young couple when they had become engaged.

They received many presents mostly because the Duke was of importance and not only at the Queen's Court.

He was well known in the Sporting world where his horses had won a great many of the most celebrated Classic races.

Lady Margaret, who had been only eighteen, had not been consulted if she wished to marry Prince Frederick.

She was merely told by her father that a marriage had been arranged, that her *fiancé* was a Crown Prince and in time she would reign over the Principality of Lucenhoff.

It was after the Prince had arrived in England and they were visiting their various relations that Lady Margaret met Captain D'Arcy Marsh.

At a party given by the Duke and Duchess of Devonshire she and Prince Frederick were the honoured guests.

There were about thirty people for dinner and afterwards a number of friends were invited to dance.

The ballroom opened out into a delightful garden sloping down from Piccadilly to Berkeley Square.

As Lady Margaret came from the ballroom with a partner, she accidentally dropped her little gold chain bag. It contained a handkerchief, a half-guinea to tip a housemaid with and a small comb.

As it fell to the ground, she gave an exclamation.

Before the elderly Statesman she had been dancing with could move, it was picked up by a young man standing nearby.

As she took it from him, she saw that he was without exception quite the most handsome man she had ever seen in her life.

"Thank you," she smiled at him shyly.

"I am honoured to be of service," he replied, "and I only hope that you will reward me by having the next dance with me."

As he spoke, the orchestra behind them in the ballroom struck up a dreamy waltz.

Lady Margaret looked apprehensively at her previous partner.

"I enjoyed our dance," he told her, "and that is the only one I shall attempt this evening. Now you go along, my dear, and enjoy yourself while you can."

Lady Margaret thanked him and turned towards the handsome man waiting impatiently at her side.

He led her up the steps and into the ballroom and, as they moved around the polished floor, he began,

"I have been wondering frantically how I could get an introduction to you and I am more grateful than I can say to your little bag!"

Lady Margaret laughed.

"I mean it," he said. "How can you be so exquisitely beautiful and yet be a real person, someone I am holding in my arms?"

The way he spoke made Lady Margaret blush.

At the same time there was a note in his voice that made a little quiver run through her.

It was something that she had never felt before, certainly not with the Prince who she had to admit to herself that she was somewhat afraid of.

He was very pompous, extremely stiff and, she thought, difficult to talk to.

She had found herself wondering ever since her engagement had been announced how she could marry a man who seemed as far away from her as if he was on top of a mountain covered in snow.

He had what her Nanny had called 'cold eyes' and she had the uncomfortable feeling that she would never be at ease with him.

She that started to dance around the room with her partner murmuring extravagant compliments in her ear, which made her heart beat even faster.

They moved perfectly in unison, which made her feel as if they were one person instead of two.

Before the dance ended he took her out of the ballroom and down the steps into the garden.

The paths were edged with fairy lights and there were Chinese lanterns swinging from the branches of the trees.

With his hand under her elbow the young man drew Lady Margaret away from the house and down the sloping lawns to where there were no lights and there was only the glimmer of the stars shining through the branches of the trees.

Then he stopped.

He stood looking down at her and, as her eyes grew accustomed to the starlight, she could see his face quite clearly.

"You will not believe this," he said in a deep voice, "but from the moment I walked into the ballroom tonight and saw you, I knew that I was in love!"

'B-but I am – sure that is – untrue," Lady Margaret objected hesitantly.

"You would know if I was lying," he replied. "I have been looking for you all my life and now that I have found you I cannot let you go!"

"You – you don't – understand," Lady Margaret whispered, "I am – engaged to be married to Prince Frederick of Lucenhoff."

"If you were engaged or married to Apollo or Zeus," her partner answered, "I would still love you. I am not a Prince. My name is D'Arcy Marsh and I am of no particular consequence to anyone."

He paused, took a deep breath and then continued,

"But whatever you may say, you were created for me and I was created for you, and now that we have at last met at last what are we going to do about it?"

It was impossible for Lady Margaret not to listen to him and not to find herself mesmerised by him to the point where she could not think.

She certainly could not tear herself away from him and they stood in the shadows of the trees for what seemed like a long time.

Then, as if it was inevitable, he kissed her.

As he put his arms around her, she did not struggle and her lips were waiting for his.

As he held her captive, she knew that this was what she had always dreamed of, wanted and believed would happen to her one day.

It was *love*, the love that she had been always told was not necessary in marriage.

"I love you and you love me whether you know it or not!" D'Arcy Marsh then claimed triumphantly.

They went back into the ballroom and it seemed that nobody had missed them.

Driving back to Nevon House in Park Lane Lady Margaret's head was spinning, her heart was beating too fast and the whole world seemed to have turned itself upside down.

She met D'Arcy again early the next morning when they were both riding in Rotten Row in Hyde Park.

He called round to see her in the afternoon when she knew that her father had an appointment.

She received him in the small cosy sitting room that the Duke used when they were alone.

She was waiting from him and, when he was announced and the door had been closed by the butler behind him, he stood gazing at her for a moment.

Then she was in his arms.

She tried to protest and she tried to say that it was wrong, but it was too late.

He was kissing her wildly, passionately and possessively and she knew that nothing else in the world mattered except for him.

It was a fortnight before D'Arcy finally persuaded her to run away with him.

She tried because she thought that it was right to tell her father that she had no wish to marry Prince Frederick.

She had always been a little frightened of her father and he had become very much more autocratic and overbearing since her mother died.

Lady Margaret was therefore trembling when she went into his study.

Her father was sitting at his desk writing and, as she came into the room, he turned and commented briefly,

"I am busy, Margaret."

"I-I want to – talk to you, Papa," Lady Margaret stammered.

"I must finish the list of guests who have to be invited to the Wedding," the Duke said irritably. "So many relations will insist on coming that there will hardly be any room for our friends!"

"B-but I want – to tell you, Papa – that I do *not* – wish to – m-marry the Prince."

For a moment what she had said did not seem to percolate through to the Duke's mind.

Then he growled,

"What did you say? What is all this about? Not marry the Prince? Of course you will marry the Prince!"

"B-but – I-I don't – love him, Papa."

The Duke put down his pen.

"Love? What has that got to do with it?" he asked. "He is a Prince. His Principality is not large, but The Palace is comfortable and you will walk with the Crowned Heads of Europe. What more can you possibly ask?"

"I want to be – in love, Papa."

"Love! *Love*!" the Duke almost shouted irritably. "Is that all women ever think about? Love will come after marriage or it should do."

"But – Papa – I-I don't – want to be m-married!"

The Duke looked at her as if he had never seen his daughter before.

"I suppose you might find someone better than Frederick, but it will not be easy and Her Majesty is delighted. Yes, delighted! I have no time for this nonsense now. Go and talk to your grandmother, if that is what is worrying you, but don't bother me."

He picked up his pen again.

Because she knew that it was hopeless to make him understand, Lady Margaret then went from the room.

When she told D'Arcy Marsh what had happened, he laughed.

"Of course your father would not understand. You are making an excellent Society marriage that will delight all your relatives."

He laughed again and went on,

"They will soon be complaining that as a Princess you will walk into dinner ahead of them and they will have to curtsy to you! Is that what you want?"

"You know I don't want it!" Lady Margaret insisted.

"Then you have to be brave, my precious one. If you stay here, you will be dragged up the aisle and once the ring is on your finger there will be no escape. Can you face that?"

He did not wait for her answer, but kissed her until the room whirled round them and they were both flying higher and higher into the sky.

Because she knew that there was no alternative, Lady Margaret packed her own trunk for the first time in her life.

She collected her jewellery and, on D'Arcy's instructions, as much money as she could obtain from her father's secretary.

"We are going to be rich, my darling, in everything but money," D'Arcy Marsh stated, "and that you will find is a fluctuating possession."

This was something Lady Margaret was to find completely and absolutely true for the rest of her married life.

D'Arcy Marsh was always truthful about himself.

He told her that he was a gambler and it was exactly what he was.

"I gamble because I enjoy it," he told her, "because I need the money and because I am not particularly clever at anything else."

He had been made a Captain in the Grenadier Guards and had received a medal for outstanding bravery in the face of an enemy.

This was awarded to him for saving his men from an ambush in India when they would otherwise have been annihilated.

He had, however, given up his life in the Army, which he had relished, because he claimed that he found it too expensive.

He preferred to be free to gamble and enjoy himself.

He visited the casinos of every country that had one.

But his love for Lady Margaret was something that he had not anticipated and he found it irresistible.

It was the love that men have sought since the beginning of time, but few are lucky enough to find.

He knew that his wife had given up everything that was familiar to her to be with him and they were rapturously happy.

It did not matter in the least when things went wrong and he lost at cards so that they had to live in cheap and uncomfortable lodgings.

They were together and nothing else was of any consequence or interest.

It was an extraordinary life for any woman, but especially for one who had been brought up in the luxury and splendour of being the daughter of a Duke.

Because Lady Margaret was so happy, she never worried whether they had the largest and most expensive suite or the smallest.

Whether they had a Villa in the South of France or a Paris attic where the floorboards creaked when walked on.

She was his wife and D'Arcy filled her eyes, her heart and her soul.

When he died suddenly, it was not only the story of her love that came to an end but also her life.

She could not live without him and, as she already had a cancerous growth in her inside, she knew anyway that there was no hope.

She therefore had very little time to make plans for her daughter.

It was not surprising, having been born of two handsome people, that Josina was beautiful with a magnetic, exciting spiritual beauty that it was said belonged to the Greek Goddesses.

Her features were perfect, her eyes very large and her skin translucent.

But it was much more than that.

She had an aura or a vibration that seemed to set her apart from other girls of her age.

She was not aware of it herself.

Her mother was so beautiful that she had never thought of herself as being in the same category.

The nuns at the Convent had shaken their heads when they wondered what was to become of her in the future.

The Mother Superior had given Sister Benedict strict instructions to take good care of her on the journey.

Lady Margaret had lain awake night after night wondering how she could bring her daughter safely to England.

Only when she remembered her widow's bonnet did she think that Josina's Guardian Angel, or perhaps her father, was helping her.

Lady Margaret was well aware that her husband's friends had looked admiringly at her lovely daughter.

Josina had never noticed it, but now she would be travelling alone and it could be a dangerous journey.

The fact that men stared at her was the reason why, before she was sixteen, Lady Margaret had insisted on sending her to the Convent School in Florence.

It was an exclusive school because it was patronised by all the aristocrats of Europe who wanted their daughters to be well and safely educated.

When D'Arcy made a coup at the *Monte Carlo Casino* one night and brought the money home in triumph, Lady Margaret had taken it saying,

"That is for Josina's education. You must not touch it because now it is no longer yours."

D'Arcy Marsh had laughed and answered her,

"Very well, my precious love, but if we have to move out into the gutter tomorrow, don't blame me!"

Lady Margaret had put her arms around his neck.

"You know I am doing the right thing," she sighed. "She is your daughter too, you know. We have to look after her."

"To which I agree," D'Arcy admitted, "although I have very little choice in the matter!"

He then kissed his wife and they had never discussed it again.

To make quite sure that there would be no difficulty about Josina's education, Lady Margaret sent the money the very next day to the Mother Superior at the Convent in Florence.

But it was nearly a year before Lady Margaret sent her daughter there. It was only because she knew that, now that Josina was no longer a child, it was going to be more and more difficult to keep men from approaching her.

She was very different from other girls of her age and so lovely that every man who looked at her stopped and looked again.

They immediately wanted to know her.

Josina had cried when she reached the Convent, but she soon began to enjoy it.

There had never been time for her to make any friends of her own age when she was with her father and mother. They always seemed to be moving on to somewhere else.

Also, amongst important people, D'Arcy Marsh, because he was a gambler, found that doors were more often than not closed against him.

His family was in fact an old one and his forebears had been Squires in Huntingdonshire for five generations.

D'Arcy was indeed a gentleman.

He had been educated at Eton and Oxford University and had then joined the Grenadier Guards because it was a family tradition to do so.

He had found it restraining and the life of a soldier could be restraining at times.

He had discovered quite by chance that he had an uncanny knack as a gambler and it was a challenge that he could not resist.

He travelled from casino to casino, from Paris to Rome and from Monte Carlo to Vienna.

As well he went from Baden-Baden to Nuremberg and at every one of these places he was warmly welcomed.

The cards and the tables would be dutifully waiting for him.

He lived a life of adventure and excitement that never became monotonous.

Just as his love for Lady Margaret survived every difficulty, every setback and every crisis, so his life as a gambler with its ups and downs continued to delight and enthral him.

The only time Lady Margaret ever had any doubts about their curious existence was when she was worrying about Josina.

Now, as she looked up at her daughter, she said faintly,

"You may – find it difficult in – England. But if the new Duke – accepts you then the – whole family will follow his example."

"And if they do not, Mama, I shall have to fend for myself," Josina pointed out.

Lady Margaret gave a little cry.

"No! You must – persuade one member of my family at least – to be kind and to take – care of you. It is – wrong and wicked that – you should – suffer for my – sins."

Josina smiled.

"Was it really such a sin, Mama, to run away with the man you loved? I think it was very romantic – and you were very happy."

"I was – very happy – very – very happy," Lady Margaret whispered.

Josina bent forward to kiss her mother's cheek.

"Don't worry about anything, Mama. I am sure you are right and that the Duke will find a member of the family who will be pleased to have me to live with them. And I hope one day I shall find someone like Papa."

It was with an effort that Lady Margaret smiled.

"That is – what I – pray for and what I shall – go on praying for – wherever I am."

She closed her eyes and lay back on her pillows exhausted.

Josina went to find the maid who looked after her mother.

An Italian woman, she was too old to take a position where she could obtain more money.

She told Josina in no uncertain terms that there was practically nothing to eat in the house.

Josina had a little money left over from her journey, which she gave to the woman and told her to go out and buy some food.

But what she felt was most important was not that she should have food but her mother.

Then she went up the stairs again.

She thought afterwards that even before she entered the room she had known what she would find.

Lady Margaret had stayed alive just long enough to tell her daughter what she wanted her to do.

Now her last task over and she had gone to join the man she loved.

CHAPTER TWO

Josina looked round the sitting room and wondered if there was anything else that she really wanted to take with her to England.

Her mother had been buried yesterday morning and she had arranged for someone to take her to Milan later in the afternoon.

And from there she could catch a fast train to carry her to France.

What had worried her, however, was that, when she was looking for the money that her mother had put on one side for the journey, she found a letter addressed to the Duke of Nevondale.

It was obviously the one that her mother had told her she had written to the Duke.

But it had not been sent.

It was addressed and Josina went down to ask the maid why it had not been posted.

"No money!" the Italian woman replied gruffly.

This meant, Josina knew, that she would arrive unannounced.

It would therefore be more difficult than it was already to find the Duke and beg for his assistance.

However, there was nothing she could do about it now and all she was concerned about was taking what she really wanted to keep with her to England.

She would leave the rest for the Italian woman to sell as she could not give her any more wages.

When she examined her mother's wardrobe, she found that Lady Margaret had already sold all the elaborate and pretty gowns that she had worn when her husband was alive.

Many of them, when he had been successful at gambling, had been very expensive and the height of fashion.

Josina could not help wondering how much she had sold them for in the small town of Pavia.

This meant that she only had the clothes that she had worn at school, which were very plain and simple, as the Mother Superior always preferred.

Then there were the two black gowns that her mother had been wearing since her father had died.

Josina could not help feeling that she would look very shabby amongst the English.

She hoped, but it was a forlorn hope, that the Duke might be generous enough to give her an allowance of some sort.

'But it is no use speculating,' she decided.

She knew that above all she must keep her promise to her mother and leave for England immediately.

She found the widow's hat that Lady Margaret had told her was in the cupboard of her bedroom.

She also found the plain black gown with the coat over it that her mother had worn at her father's funeral.

She put it on, feeling the tears come into her eyes as she remembered how happy and carefree they had been as long as they had both been alive.

She could not bear to think now of the senseless way of how her father had become involved in a duel.

It was with a man who he had won a great deal of money from.

Because the man had been angry at being a loser and had been drinking heavily as well, he had insulted D'Arcy Marsh by saying loudly that he had cheated.

The most sensible thing that her father could have done, Josina thought, was to have merely walked away, realising that the man was drunk.

Instead of which at midnight they had fought a duel.

D'Arcy Marsh had received a bullet just above his heart, which had killed him instantly.

It had completely broken her mother's heart and from that moment on they had a struggle to keep alive.

It was unfortunate that D'Arcy Marsh had had a run of bad luck previous to his encounter with the man from whom he had won quite a considerable fortune.

In the excitement of the duel, most of the money had mysteriously disappeared and there was no one present to say how much D'Arcy Marsh had actually won.

Lady Margaret had received a very small sum instead of what would have kept them comfortably for months.

Now Josina thought back at how everything had happened so quickly, but she had been at school and only learnt from her mother what had happened on the fateful day.

She thought that their Guardian Angels had deserted them at a crucial moment when Lady Margaret was already ill.

She needed expensive doctors and expensive appetising food.

Her mother had, however, after the funeral sent her straight back to the Convent and she had not realised how bad things really were.

Now she had discovered that everything of value had been sold and there was, as the Italian maid had pointed out to her so forcefully to her, practically nothing left.

She felt that in some ways she was glad to leave the small, rather dingy, little house behind.

Although it was frightening to leave Italy, it was too full of memories of her father and mother.

She felt exactly the same about France.

They had always loved being in Paris and there had been times in the past when D'Arcy Marsh had won night after night at *baccarat*.

Then they had lived, as Josina had commented, like Kings and Queens.

Now she was very conscious of how shabby her luggage appeared and her reflection in the mirror was of a strange woman in deep mourning.

She was determined, however, to obey her mother's instructions.

When she left for Milan, she realised that this was the beginning of a strange frightening adventure.

It might, or it might not, end in disaster.

It was only when she was in the train that she recognised how wise her mother had been to make her wear a widow's hat with a veil over her face.

The porter at the Station found her a good window seat facing the engine in a First Class compartment.

He put her two trunks in the guard's van and graciously accepted her tip, which was not a very large one,.

'Mama was clever,' Josina thought to herself. 'I would never have imagined anything so subtle as that I should travel as a widow!'

Her mother's Wedding ring was on her finger and she glanced at it once or twice, as she wondered if the day would ever come when she would wear a Wedding ring that she was entitled to.

All the girls at school had talked endlessly about love.

Many of the more aristocratic pupils had known that their marriages would be arranged for them by their fathers.

They had accepted that they would be married to a suitable man, whether they loved him, or not.

As the train sped on over the fertile land of France, Josina vowed that she would never marry unless she loved the man in the same way that her mother had so overwhelmingly loved her father.

She was intelligent and perceptive enough to realise that the love of her parents for each other had made everywhere, however poor and sordid, a place of sublime beauty.

They were so happy together that their love vibrated round them until she herself became a part of it.

'That is what I want to find one day,' she thought to herself.

She prayed that somehow she would be fortunate enough to find the 'man of her dreams'.

*

It was a long journey and she had to change trains at Paris.

When eventually she reached Calais, there was a two hour wait before the Steamer arrived to carry her across the English Channel to Dover.

As she had a First Class ticket, she was found a comfortable seat in the Saloon.

The sea was surprisingly calm and so very few passengers suffered from *mal de mer*.

Josina had, of course, slept two nights on the train and they arrived at Dover at about midday.

She had never been to England before, but her mother had talked about it so often that she felt as if everything was familiar to her.

Lady Margaret had also written down exactly how she should proceed to the family seat, Nevon Hall.

It involved two changes of trains before Josina arrived at the Halt that was used only by the Duke and his close family.

There the train stopped as she had previously arranged with the guard.

Josina stepped out and was aware that, if her mother's letter had been posted as she had meant it to be, the Duke might have sent a carriage to meet her.

As it was, when she asked how she could reach Nevon Hall, the old porter in charge of the Halt scratched his head.

"I don't rightly know, ma'am," he said. "It be two mile from 'ere and there be no carriage waitin' for you."

"Then what can – I do?" Josina asked him nervously.

"Praps Farmer Giles'll drop you orf," the porter offered finally. "I'll find out for you."

He went away and, when he had gone, Josina walked into the waiting room.

Despite the fact that it was very small there were several comfortable chairs and a table. And there was also a looking glass hanging on one wall.

As she looked at her reflection, she had a sudden idea.

Her journey was ended and her widow's bonnet had protected her exactly as her mother had planned.

But now, when she arrived at Nevon Hall, she must be herself.

Deftly she threw back the veil from her face and, draping it round the bonnet to which it was attached, she tied it in a bow at the back.

It made her look very different from the way she had looked all the time she had been journeying through Italy and France.

Now, with her golden hair shining beneath the small brim, she looked who she really was, a very young girl in mourning.

She had just finished arranging her new headgear when the porter came back.

For a moment he stared at her in astonishment.

Then, because he was too polite to be personal, he announced,

"Farmer Giles'll drop you and your luggage at The Hall. It baint be more than 'alf a mile out of 'is way."

"I am very grateful," Josina smiled. "Thank you very much."

The porter placed her trunks in Farmer Giles's cart and she tipped him.

She thought with a little pang as she did so that she was now left with less than ten shillings.

It was all she possessed in the world.

She had changed what French and Italian money she had left at Calais while she was waiting for the Steamer to arrive.

She was wondering as she sat on the high cart beside the farmer what would happen if the Duke refused to accept her.

And she would then have to leave The Hall as soon as she arrived.

She suddenly felt very frightened as the farmer's horse moved comparatively quickly down the narrow lane from the Halt.

Then she started praying desperately,

'Please God – let him be – kind to me. Please – God, let me – stay here.'

She had visions of herself having to spend the night in a ditch. Or perhaps, if she was not fortunate enough to hitch a lift, to stay in the little waiting room at the Halt.

Even if she did that she did not know if she would have enough money to carry her back to London.

Then, when she was there, how would she manage with nothing to sell or pawn, except for her mother's Wedding ring?

She had remembered to take that off after she had changed what she wore on her head.

She put it inside the black handbag she carried that had also been her mother's.

She felt grateful that the farmer was not in the least talkative.

They drove in silence until, as they turned a corner, Josina saw on the other side of the road a high brick wall,

She recalled now her mother telling her that it enclosed the Park at Nevon Hall.

She was not mistaken.

A short while afterwards the farmer turned his horse in through two large wrought iron gates with two imposing lodges on either side of them.

Now they were on the gravel drive.

Josina heard her heart beating frantically and her lips were dry.

At the same time she could not avoid taking in a deep breath with a little murmur of excitement at her first sight of Nevon Hall.

Her mother had described it to her so often and Josina therefore felt that she would in any case have recognised it.

It had first been designed by Inigo Jones and then added to by the Adam brothers.

There were, as her mother had told her, statues on the roof besides the flagstaff, which was in fact the first thing that Josina was looking for.

Her mother had told her that, when the Duke was in residence, his flag flew proudly from the roof and it was how everybody knew that he was at home.

It had, of course, crossed her mind, not once but a dozen times, that when she arrived the Duke might not be there.

She would then have to beg the servants to allow her to stay for the night or until they could communicate with His Grace.

If only her mother's letter had been posted, as Lady Margaret had intended!

Josina felt that everything then would have been so much easier.

Instead she now had to explain who she was to a man who, whether he was the Head of the Family or not, might easily resent her intrusion unannounced.

"'Ere we be," Farmer Giles said as his horse crossed the bridge over the lake. "Shall I set you down, miss, at the front door?"

Josina knew, as she had not been met, that he was wondering whether the servants' entrance would be more correct.

"The front door, if you please," she replied quietly. "I am very grateful indeed to you for – bringing me here. It would have been – a long way to walk."

She thought that he might laugh at the idea, but he remarked seriously,

"Too far for a lady like yourself."

He drew up his horse outside a long flight of impressive stone steps.

On either side there was a stone figure holding a heraldic shield that Lady Margaret had told her daughter was the family Coat of Arms.

Josina opened her bag.

"What shall I pay you for – your kindness?" she asked Farmer Giles.

"I wants nothin'," he answered. "I've not gorn far out of me way and I be glad to 'ave bin of service."

Josina thanked him profusely and shook him by the hand.

She was thinking how her mother had told her that in England, unlike many other countries, people liked to shake one's hand on every possible occasion.

She climbed down from the carriage, aware as she did so that a footman had appeared at the top of the steps.

He came down towards her and Josina asked him,

"Would you be kind enough to lift down my two trunks from the back of the cart?"

She saw the surprise on the footman's face, but she walked up the steps to the front door.

As she reached it, she saw an elderly man who was obviously the butler coming across the hall.

She stood still, waiting until he reached her.

Then she said,

"May I please see – the Duke of Nevondale."

"Is His Grace expecting you, madam?" the butler enquired.

"I am afraid not," Josina replied, "but I need to see him on a very important matter."

"Will you give me your name, madam?" the butler asked.

It was then Josina realised that he was looking at her in a very strange manner.

"My name," she told him, "is Miss Josina Marsh."

The butler gave an exclamation.

Then he said,

"You can't be! But you must be – Lady Margaret's daughter!"

Josina's eyes brightened.

"Yes, I am. Do you remember my mother?"

"I knew it, knew it soon as I set eyes on you," the butler became expansive. "You look just as her Ladyship did when I first comes here as boot boy."

Now Josina smiled.

"I am so glad you remember her," she smiled.

There was a little pause before the butler said,

"And, as you're in black, miss, has her Ladyship passed away?"

Josina nodded.

For a moment it was difficult to speak because she was so touched that someone remembered her mother.

The mere fact that the butler did so made her not so afraid and apprehensive.

"I'm Hichins," he said. "Her Ladyship would remember me if she was here with you."

"She *did* remember you," Josina answered. "She spoke about you and some of the other staff who were here when she ran away."

The butler shook his grey head.

"It were a sad day for us all when her Ladyship left," he volunteered. "And now, miss, you want to see His Grace."

"Yes, please," Josina replied. "He did not know that I would be arriving here because my mother was so ill that she failed to post the letter that she had written to him."

"You come this way, miss," Hichins suggested.

He walked ahead along the corridor and opened a door into a room that Josina knew immediately was her grandfather's study.

It was just as her mother had described it to her with heavy red velvet curtains over the windows and a flat topped Regency desk with gold feet.

The pictures on the walls were by Stubbs, Herring Senior and other artists who specialised in horses and the sofas and chairs were covered in red leather.

Josina remembered how her mother had told her that it was in this room that she had tried to tell her father, the Duke, that she could not marry Prince Frederick of Lucenhoff.

"Now you wait here, miss," Hichins was saying, "and I'll tell His Grace, who's dressing for dinner, that you've arrived. It'll be a surprise for him, as you surprised me!"

He did not wait for Josina to reply, but hurried away and left her alone.

Now, because she was in her mother's home, Josina felt that she was near to her and guiding her in what she should say.

She was helping in the way that she would have done had she been alive.

'It is going to be more difficult, Mama,' she said in her heart, 'because the Duke has not had your letter. But I will give it to him to read and then perhaps he will think of me more kindly than just someone who has dropped in in an unexpected manner, which would undoubtedly be a nuisance for him.'

She drew the letter, which she had carried carefully, from her handbag and stood trembling a little with her back to the fireplace.

As it was summer, there was no fire and the hearth was full of plants making a vivid patch of colour.

It made Josina think how beautiful the gardens that her mother had talked about would be.

She was praying she would be able to see them.

Just as she wanted to see the rest of the house before the Duke sent her away, perhaps to some other relation.

At the same time she was hoping fervently that he would not be angry because she was there.

It seemed to her as if she had waited for a very long time.

Then the door opened and the Duke came in.

Josina had not been certain what she expected.

Her mother had never seen the distant cousin who had inherited the title so all she knew about him was that his name was 'Rollo'.

Because she was so frightened when he appeared and the door closed behind him, for a moment it was impossible to look at him.

The whole room seemed to be swimming around her.

Then, as he advanced towards her, he said in a deep and what she thought was a rather cold voice,

"I understand that you are Lady Margaret Marsh's daughter and that you wish to see me."

"Yes, Your Grace," Josina said remembering to drop him a small curtsey. "I-I have brought you – this letter."

She was aware as she held it out to him that her hand was trembling.

The Duke took it from her.

Then, as he opened it and read it slowly, she was able to look at him.

He was, she thought, surprisingly good-looking and she had somehow expected him to have a stern rather hard face.

Instead of which she thought that he looked almost raffish with dark hair growing back from a square forehead and a firm chin. His features, she knew without being told, were aristocratic.

|Equally there was something young and rather glamorous about him.

It did not fit in with her idea of a powerful and pompous Duke who was the Head of a great Family.

The Duke carefully read the letter that Lady Margaret had written to him in a rather unsteady hand.

Then he looked up at Josina and said,

"Your mother says in this letter that she is dying and I presume that is why you have come here."

"I-I know Mama has – asked you to – accept me into the family – and to find someone who will – look after me," Josina answered.

"Yes, I understand that," the Duke said, "but I think I should have received this letter by post."

"That is what – Mama intended, but the – servant who was told to post it had – no money and so the – only thing – I could do was to bring it – with me."

"If you had no money, then how did you manage to get here?" the Duke enquired.

"Mama put aside a certain – amount just for the – journey," Josina said, "and I followed her – instructions that, as soon as the – funeral had taken place, I was to – come here. But, of course – you were not – expecting me."

"Well, you are here," the Duke remarked, "and I suppose we must do something about it."

Josina's eyes lit up.

'Y-you mean – you will help me?"

The Duke smiled.

"You give me little alternative. I can hardly send you away when you tell me that you have no money and, according to your mother, have never been to England before."

"That is – true," Josina agreed, "you – know that – Mama could – not come back."

She spoke a little tentatively, wondering what his feelings would be about the scandal that her mother had caused.

To her relief the Duke smiled.

"If I have been told the story of your mother's elopement once," he said, "I have been told it a hundred times. It certainly gave the family something to talk about! It will undoubtedly be an excuse to repeat and repeat it again and again when they learn that you are here!"

"I think it was – very brave of Mama to – do such – a thing," Josina commented a little defiantly.

"I agree with you," the Duke answered, "and I have often wondered, ever since I heard the story, whether she found it worthwhile."

"I have never known – two people happier than my father and mother, until he – d-died," Josina stammered.

"And your father is also dead," the Duke said. "Your mother does not say how he died."

"He was – killed in a duel," Josina replied.

"Always the dramatic!" the Duke declared, but his eyes were twinkling. "I can see that your arrival is going to cause the family chatterboxes to start talking until we are all quite deafened by the sound!"

Josina gave him a little smile before she asked,

"You are not – angry with me for – coming here?"

"Angry? Of course not," the Duke replied. "And, as your mother points out in her letter, I am the Head of the Family and responsible for everyone, good, bad or indifferent."

He glanced at the clock on the mantelpiece.

"As it is now nearly dinnertime," he said, "I think perhaps you would like to wash and change. I will give you exactly twenty minutes. Do you think you can manage?"

"Of course I can," Josina replied, "and thank you – very very – much for not sending me away, as I was half – afraid you – might do."

The Duke spread out his hands.

"Away – to where?" he asked, "and Hichins tells me that you came here in the farmer's cart. I imagine that he is not waiting outside in case you need him to take you back!"

"No, and thank you – again," Josina sighed. "I have been so very – frightened – all the time I was – coming here."

"We will talk about your future tomorrow," the Duke suggested. "Now, please hurry because I am hungry and so are my guests. As your mother will have told you, a chef, if he is any good, does not like to keep his food waiting until it is overcooked."

He spoke in a way that made Josina give another little laugh.

Then, as he opened the study door for her to pass through it, they walked quickly into the hall.

Hichins was waiting and the Duke ordered him,

"Take Miss Marsh upstairs, Hichins. I have given her twenty minutes to change for dinner."

"Very good, Your Grace," Hichins replied. "I've already sent Miss Marsh's luggage up to Mrs. Meadows."

The Duke did not wait to reply.

He merely walked across the hall to another door from where, as it was opened for him by a footman, Josina heard the sound of voices.

His guests had obviously already come downstairs for dinner.

She therefore quickly followed Hichins up the stairs knowing full well that she must try not to keep anyone waiting.

On the landing was a very impressive figure dressed in rustling black silk with a chatelaine at her waist.

This, she was immediately aware, was the housekeeper, Mrs. Meadows, and Josina knew that she had been at The Hall when her mother was a girl.

As she held out her hand, Mrs. Meadows said,

"It might be her Ladyship herself! You're so like her, miss, that I'd know who you were wherever I saw you."

"Mama often spoke about you," Josina told her.

As she spoke, she felt the tears come into her eyes.

Everything was so different from what she had feared it would be.

She was in her mother's home, two of the servants remembered her and the Duke had been kind to her.

However, at the moment the only thing that mattered was that she must concentrate on not keeping him waiting.

As they went into a large and very attractive bedroom, she saw that two housemaids were already unpacking her trunks.

*

Josina had changed into the one black evening gown that her mother had owned and was downstairs in under fifteen minutes.

The two housemaids and Mrs. Meadows had helped her into it and, because they were all aware that time was passing, they had hardly talked as they poured out water for her to wash in.

They found what she was to wear in one of her trunks and helped her out of the clothes that she had travelled in.

Josina wished that she could have a bath, but she knew that was impossible in such a short time.

She was well aware from what her mother had told her that the hot water had to be brought upstairs by the footmen and the housemaids meanwhile brought in the bath and put it on the hearthrug. They then poured the water from the hot and cold brass cans until it was the right temperature.

Now that her face and hands were clean Mrs. Meadows skilfully arranged her hair.

Taking her handkerchief from one of the housemaids, Josina ran across the room to the door, which was opened for her by the other maid.

She hurried down the great staircase and Hichins smiled at her approvingly as she reached the hall.

"You've done it, miss," he whispered.

She felt that he was as pleased as if she had run a cross-country race or ridden round a Racecourse in record time.

He walked briskly ahead of her to the door into what she was to learn was the drawing room.

Opening the door he announced in stentorian tones,

"Miss Josina Marsh, Your Grace."

Josina went in.

There were six people in the room and the Duke moved towards her looking, she had to admit, very impressive in his evening clothes.

"I commend you," he greeted her, "on being exceedingly punctual. Let me introduce you to my friends."

It was only when they were seated at the dining room table that Josina was able to scrutinise the party as she had felt too shy to do so when the Duke had introduced her.

She recognised at once that she was an extra uninvited woman and therefore not likely to be welcome.

She was aware that this was the truth when she saw the woman on the Duke's right looking at her in a somewhat hostile manner.

Josina realised that she was French and, as the evening wore on, she learned that she was the Comtesse de Soissons, and wife of one of the Attachés at the French Embassy.

Because Josina had travelled with her father and mother to all the most glamorous and exciting places in Europe she had grown perceptive about people.

She was not easily deceived by what they pretended to be rather than what they were.

She was aware almost immediately that the Comtesse and the two other ladies present were the sort of women who her mother most disliked.

This was because invariably they flirted with and pursued her father.

Lady Margaret would never go to the casino with him, but naturally they met those who he gambled with at other times.

Josina had grown to realise that her mother stiffened when an extremely glamorous woman, usually over-painted and powdered, would put a hand on her father's arm and say coyly,

"Captain D'Arcy, how lovely to see you. And congratulations on your success last night."

She would talk in a cooing seductive voice flashing her eyes as she did so.

Although it was obvious that her father was not in the least interested in these women, they did everything they could to hold his attention.

It was that sort of woman and the men who were with them who made Lady Margaret glad to leave somewhere like Monte Carlo.

Inevitably, however, the same type would always be waiting for them wherever they went next.

Because of what might be called a 'cosmopolitan education', although Josina had been to a Convent, she was well aware that her mother would not have approved of the Comtesse or of the other two ladies in the party.

They were all three of them extremely attractive in their own way.

But the mascara was too heavy on their eyelashes and the salve was too red on their lips. And their gowns were too low in the front and too elaborate for a dinner party in the country.

But the men present were gentlemen there was no doubt about that.

But when they looked at her, Josina knew that there was an expression in their eyes that had made her mother hurry her off to the Convent in Florence just before she was sixteen.

Josina was sure that it would never have occurred to her mother that the Duke would be someone young and what her father would often describe as a roué.

She had heard him say once to her mother when she had criticised a man who he was friendly with,

"My dearest, you find them everywhere. And what would women do if there were not roués to flatter them and, of course, enjoy every flirtatious glance they give so beguilingly?"

Lady Margaret had known that he was teasing her, but she had replied,

"Is that what you want, D'Arcy?"

Her father had laughed and put his arms around her mother.

"You know what I want is what I have and what I will never lose," he answered. "And I am delighted, my darling, that you still love me enough to be jealous!"

He had then kissed his wife passionately until they both forgot that Josina was in the room.

Now she remembered that her mother had been nervous of all the glamorous exciting women they saw everywhere they went. And they inevitably gravitated towards her father because he was so good-looking.

As dinner progressed and the wine glasses were filled and refilled, the voices and laughter in the dining room grew louder.

While the Comtesse became more and more intimate with the Duke continually touching his arm and his hand with her thin fingers.

Josina knew that this was something that her mother had not anticipated she would find in her old home.

'And of course,' she now told herself, 'I am very much *de trop*.'

With this in mind, when dinner came to an end and the ladies withdrew into the drawing room, she turned quickly to the Comtesse and said,

"I hope you will not think me rude – if I retire to bed. Having travelled for three days – I am actually very tired."

She saw what she thought was an expression of relief in the Comtesse's dark eyes.

'Of course, poor child," she replied, "you must have your beauty sleep. Go upstairs at once and I will make your apologies to our host who I know will understand."

"I am sure he will understand anything you tell him," one of the women interposed rather pointedly.

"Why not," the Comtesse said. "What I tell him is what he wants to hear."

She was speaking in French, but, of course, Josina understood and she understood too the pointed innuendo behind the words.

She said 'goodnight' to the three ladies, who were obviously delighted to see her go and went upstairs to her room.

She was not surprised to find that Mrs. Meadows was there.

"I thought, bein' that you'd been travellin' for so long, Miss Josina," she said, "you'd come to bed early. It's ever so sensible of you."

"I am indeed very tired," Josina confessed. "It's not easy to sleep sitting up in a train all night."

"It's something I hope never to do," Mrs. Meadows said. "Now come along, miss, let me help you off with your gown. The sooner you close your eyes the better."

She spoke as a Nanny might have done and Josina was only too glad to let her help her into her nightgown.

"Now just you goes to sleep and forget everythin' until tomorrow mornin'," Mrs. Meadows advised her as Josina climbed into bed. "Things aren't the same as when your mother was here and that's the truth. But we'll talk about that in the mornin'."

"Are they very changed?" Josina asked her.

"They are in some ways," Mrs. Meadows replied, "and not for the better. But His Grace is carryin' on the estate as your grandfather had it and takes some of his responsibilities seriously."

"Then I hope he will feel that – I am one of them," Josina remarked.

Mrs. Meadows pressed her lips together.

"I'm hopin' for your dear mother's sake, God rest her soul, that you will go to one of the family who will look after you as her Ladyship'd wish. It's not right that you should be here, although I'm not tellin' you why."

Mrs. Meadows moved towards the door.

"God bless you, Miss Josina," she said, "and may the angels look after you."

She went from the room as she spoke and Josina was in darkness.

As she closed her eyes, she was thinking over what the housekeeper had said to her.

She could easily understand her being shocked by the Comtesse and the other women.

They were certainly not what her mother would have expected to find in her home and on such familiar terms with the Duke.

'It's certainly surprising,' Josina thought, just before she fell into a deep sleep.

CHAPTER THREE

Josina awoke early and, with a little feeling of delight, realised that she was in her mother's old home.

It was so exciting that she jumped out of bed and ran across the room to the window.

The morning sun was shining on the lake and turning it to a delightful gold and the swans were swimming underneath an arch of the bridge.

It was all just as her mother had told her it would be.

She thought that nothing could be lovelier than the great oak trees with the stags resting beneath them and the shadows cast by the sunlight seemed mysterious over the long drive.

'How could Mama have left all this behind?' she asked herself.

And then she knew that her mother never regretted for one tiny instant running away with the man she loved.

Nevertheless her ancestral home had always held a very special place in her heart.

'I must explore everything here,' Josina thought, 'just in case the Duke sends me away at once to some relative.'

She hoped that it would not be in London because she had seen so many Cities, but had never been able to stay long in the country as she would have liked.

She dressed herself quickly in one of the plain gowns that she had worn at school and combed her hair into a bun at the back of her neck.

Opening the door quietly, she went down the stairs trying not to appear to be in too much of a hurry.

The housemaids were already brushing the floor in the drawing room and the footmen in their shirtsleeves were tidying the hall.

They looked at her in surprise and then smiled when they realised who she was.

"Good morning!" Josina said. "It is such a lovely day that I want to be out in the sunshine."

She did not wait for the footmen to reply, but walked out through the open front door and down the long flight of steps.

If the house had seemed impressive yesterday evening, it was even more so today.

Now she could look around her not feeling afraid and her hands were no longer trembling.

She decided that she would leave the lake until last.

She then went round the back of the house where she was sure there would be flower gardens, a bowling green and a cascade, just as her mother had described to her detail.

She was not disappointed.

Everything was there, even more beautiful and in fact bigger than she had imagined it would be.

The flowers filling the beds were breathtaking and she knew that nothing she had seen abroad, even in Paris or Vienna, could compare with the beauty of Nevon Hall.

The bees and butterflies were hovering over every flower and the birds were singing happily in the trees.

When she went from the garden into a shrubbery, she heard rabbits and other small creatures hurrying away in the undergrowth.

There was a fountain playing in the centre of a large green lawn.

The water was being thrown up into the sunshine and it looked as if a thousand rainbows were falling into the exquisitely sculpted basin.

Josina was standing looking up at the fountain, her head thrown back and the sunshine on her golden hair when she became aware that there was someone walking across the lawn towards her.

As she turned, she realised at once that it was the Duke.

He came up to her and she looked at him enquiringly, wondering if he would rebuke her for having come out alone.

"I see that you are admiring the fountain," he began. "I am sure that your mother must have told you how many centuries it has been here."

"Yes, she did," Josina replied, "but it is even more beautiful than I had expected."

The Duke smiled.

"That is what I thought about Nevon Hall the first time I came here."

"And did you expect then to own it?" Josina asked him.

He shook his head.

"I had no idea that I would ever be so fortunate with three of the line in front of me. I expected to be just 'another cousin' for the rest of my life."

Josina smiled then she enquired,

"And now?"

"Now I think I am a very fortunate man," the Duke answered. "I find Nevon more beautiful every time I come home."

Josina thought to herself that this was certainly not how she expected him to think or to speak.

As she looked at him enquiringly, he said,

"Are you, like all the Nevons, looking on me as an intruder?"

"No, of course not, although naturally Mama was very upset when both her brothers were killed, but she was always sorry that she had not met you."

"And I would like to have met her," the Duke said. "I am told by the servants that you are very like her. They also told me that she was very beautiful."

It took Josina a moment to realise that he had paid her a compliment.

Then she responded quickly,

"No one could be more beautiful than Mama and that is what my father always said. He travelled a great deal and had met nearly all the great beauties of Europe."

"I have always been interested in your father," the Duke stated. "Did he really make a living entirely from gambling?"

"We had no other source of income and, as you are I am sure aware, gambling is a gamble. Sometimes we were very rich, sometimes very poor."

The Duke laughed.

"That must have been somewhat disconcerting at times."

"It did not seem to matter," Josina said. "Mama and Papa were so happy together that they really did not notice whether they were in some very expensive and luxurious hotel or rather dingy lodgings."

She was looking back into the past as she spoke.

The Duke watching her closely thought that he had never known a woman to have such expressive eyes.

He suddenly felt as if he could almost see what Josina was thinking.

Then, as he realised that in talking about her father and mother, she was missing them desperately, he said,

"I suggest we go in for breakfast and I expect when we have eaten you would like to see the stables."

"I would love to!" Josina exclaimed. "I feel sure that you own some very fine horses, just as my grandfather did."

"I am hoping that I will be as successful on the Racecourse as he was," the Duke replied, "but the competition is far greater today than it used to be."

They talked about horses as they walked back to the house.

When they went into the breakfast room, Josina was surprised to see that there was nobody else there.

Everything was laid out just as her mother had told her it used to be.

There were a number of silver dishes on the sideboard and they waited on themselves, which was traditional.

She found it difficult with such a choice of dishes to choose which looked the most appertising.

The Duke carried her plate and set it down on the table next to his place.

As he sat down at the head of the table, Josina asked,

"Have your friends gone riding or are they just late for breakfast? I always believed that people in England ate very early."

"It depends on what time they go to bed," the Duke smiled.

Josina thought it strange that, in the country and with such a small party, people should be so late for any meal.

She knew that it would be considered impolite to comment and so she sat down to eat the fish and eggs that she had put on her plate.

"Can this really be your first visit to England?" the Duke asked her unexpectedly.

"You know that my mother could not return after the family had been so angry with her," Josina replied.

"I know that," the Duke said, "but it does seem strange that, looking so English and apparently knowing English ways, you should have stayed abroad for all these years."

"I was at a Convent School for the last two," Josina informed him.

"A Convent?" the Duke queried.

He seemed so surprised that she could not help saying,

"Did you expect me to be leading a wild life because my father was a gambler?"

"I am sure it is what our relatives thought," the Duke replied after a moment, "and I think they will be extremely surprised at how different you are from what they might have expected."

"Am I so very different?" Josina asked.

She thought that the Duke hesitated before he said.

"I can understand now that because you have been educated in a Convent you are so *unsophisticated*."

He hesitated over the last word and Josina thought that he was going to say 'innocent' and then changed his mind.

"We were certainly very strictly guarded there," she told the Duke, "and the other pupils would have been shocked had they known that my father's gambling paid my fees!"

She did not add that in order to get her into the Convent her mother had used her title.

After she had run away, she had called herself 'Mrs. Marsh' and she did not use her title unless there was some very good reason for doing so.

She was well aware that she would have been treated very differently if people were aware that she was the daughter of a Duke.

Yet she had no desire to be anything but her husband's wife. She used his name and took great pains not to draw attention to herself.

It was only when she wanted to send Josina to the most respected Convent in Florence that she wrote using her title and making it abundantly clear who her family was.

The Mother Superior had indeed been impressed.

Yet later, when she had been told about Josina's father being a gambler, she had said nothing about it.

Nor did she alter in any respect the way that Josina was treated.

Now, after what the Duke had said, it struck Josina for the first time that, having been shocked at her mother running away, they would expect her to be contaminated by the life that her parents led.

They would be aware that on the Continent her father moved in what was considered to be a 'fast' Society.

No doubt they expected that she had mixed with those people too.

It was certainly a Society that was always talked about in England as being particularly outrageous.

Ever since the casino had opened in Monte Carlo the Clergy of every nation had denounced it as a place of evil, 'a Hell on Earth'.

There were letters in the English newspapers deploring the fact that any Englishman would set foot in such a den of iniquity.

Josina could well remember her father reading them to her mother and laughing.

"Does anybody really believe all this nonsense?" he had asked once. "People gamble with their money it is true, but I know of places in London which are far worse in every way to what one encounters in Monte Carlo or in any other City for that matter."

"The Bishops of the Church of England have made up their minds that gambling is wicked and evil," Lady Margaret exclaimed.

"I think they would find far more wickedness in Piccadilly Circus," D'Arcy Marsh retorted. "Or in St. James's for that matter. In fact, let me tell you – "

Before he could say anything more Lady Margaret put a finger to her lips and glanced to where Josina was sitting quietly in a corner with a book in her lap.

However she was obviously at the moment listening to what her father was saying.

He had thrown *The Times* down on the floor and turned to his daughter,

"Remember this, Josina, if you are going to condemn anything, make quite certain that you have the right to do so and it is not a case of 'the pot calling the kettle black'."

Josina thought at the time how ridiculous the crusade against the casino at Monte Carlo was.

She knew that the stories of people losing all their money were grossly exaggerated. Also very few men were known to have committed suicide if they lost disastrously.

"The Bishops talk as if half the population are throwing themselves into the sea," her father said once. "I was talking to the Prefect of Police the other night and he says that they have had only one suicide in six months and the newspaper headlines have little relation to the truth."

As Josina grew older, however, she realised that people in England particularly were really shocked at the fashion for gambling.

Yet it took place in Hamburg, Marienbad, Baden-Baden and a great number of other places in Europe besides Monte Carlo.

She avidly read the English newspapers that her father and mother bought wherever they went. She also read the French newspapers, which laughed at what was reported and called the English a lot of 'stuffy old Puritans'.

Now she could not help thinking that perhaps it was a mistake for her to have come to England if because of her father she was to be ostracised.

Or worse still have him disparaged and criticised by people who had never known him.

He gambled because it amused him as other men played polo, rode in races or shot wild birds.

He was generous, in fact often too generous to those who were down on their luck.

He had never told her mother, but they had heard from other people.

If he had won a great deal of money from a young man who was making a fool of himself, he would give him back some of the money that he had lost and tell him to be more sensible another time.

Josina was, however, well aware what the Church said about the casinos where her father spent so much of his time.

She was intelligent enough now to understand that her Nevon relatives would expect her to have somehow become like the overdressed over-painted women who frequented such places.

She knew only too well that they frequented casinos hoping to pick the pockets of any man who had managed a good win at the tables.

Once again the Duke knew what she was thinking and he said,

"You must not let it worry you anymore. I know when our relatives meet you that they will be surprised and, of course, delighted that you are exactly what your mother was like before she ran away."

"Did they expect Mama – to have changed?" Josina asked him.

"I think you will find the older generation believe that you 'cannot touch pitch without being defiled'," the Duke answered.

His eyes were twinkling as he spoke.

Then he added,

"And I think you will find that I have been put into almost the same category as your father."

Josina was startled.

Her eyes widened and she asked,

"You? But – why?"

Then, as she spoke, she remembered how the Comtesse had looked at him last night and the way that the other women who were staying in the house had behaved at dinner.

"Now what we have to decide," the Duke said in a different tone, "is what I am to do about you."

Even as he spoke the door opened and the two men who were guests came into the breakfast room.

Josina already knew that one was called 'Harry' and the other 'Johnnie', but she had no idea what their other names were.

The Duke looked up as they entered.

"You are late!" he berated them.

"Are you surprised?" Harry asked. "You know only too well what Doris is like!"

Even as he spoke he reached the table and saw Josina.

Then, as he realised that he had made a *faux pas*, he said quickly,

"I think the trouble is, Rollo, that your wine last night was too potent and I now need some exercise to clear my brain."

"That is what I was thinking as well," Johnnie said, "so what about those horses we keep hearing about that are are the best in England?"

"I thought you would want to ride," the Duke smiled, "and I have already ordered one for myself in half-an-hour."

As he spoke, he looked at Josina and said,

"Would you like to ride with us, Josina? Or are you tired after your long journey?"

"I would love to ride!" Josina replied. "Mama used to tell me about the private Racecourse you have here and how she used to take part in the Steeplechases that her father arranged every year."

"Oddly enough I am to attend one today," the Duke declared, "and I have already been told by not one person on the estate but at least a hundred exactly what is expected when I have one here."

Johnnie laughed.

"You must certainly keep up the traditions and I shall be delighted to compete in today's Steeplechase, if you will provide me with a horse."

"Of course," the Duke agreed, "but I think that my Steeplechase should wait until the weather grows cooler. However we might have a Point-to-Point next month."

"That is certainly a good idea," Harry approved. "And I have a horse that I would like to bring down, Rollo, which I will bet is the equal of anything you have here in your stable."

"That is indeed a challenge," the Duke laughed.

It was then he saw that Josina was listening and he added,

"If you are going to ride with us, you had better go and get ready."

Josina gave a cry of dismay.

"I did not bring a habit with me. I did not ride when we were in Florence and I have nothing to wear."

She did not say that she had found when she had looked round the house that her mother had sold not only her father's riding clothes, breeches and boots but also her own.

She had also sold the habit that Josina had worn when they had lived in Vienna.

There she had ridden in the famous Spanish Riding School and had been commended as being an excellent equestrienne.

She had grown out of her habit while she had been at the Convent and she certainly heeded a larger size in boots.

The Duke, seeing the disappointment in her eyes, suggested,

"I am certain you will find that Mrs. Meadows will have your mother's riding clothes tucked away somewhere. She has never been known to throw anything away!"

He paused and then continued,

"In fact I am told that there are clothes in the attics to supply a dozen orphanages, but she will not part with them."

Josina laughed.

"I remember Mama saying that everything in the house was kept from one generation to another. But, may I really go and ask her if she has something I can wear?"

"Of course," the Duke said, "but you had better hurry in case we go without you!"

He was teasing, but Josina gave a little cry of horror and ran from the room.

When she had gone, Harry said,

"You realise, Rollo, that your cousin is far too beautiful for any man's peace of mind! You had better have her strictly chaperoned or she may find herself in trouble, especially having had a father like D'Arcy Marsh."

"She has just been telling me that she has spent the last year or so in a Convent School," the Duke replied.

"Good Heavens!" Johnnie exclaimed. "That is unexpected. But I suppose if her father and mother were dancing the 'gay fandango' in every casino in Europe, they found a child somewhat of a burden on their hands."

The Duke rose from the table.

"I have always thought," he said, "it extremely unfair that the Bible decrees that '*the sins of the fathers shall be visited upon the children*'."

"*Unto the third and fourth generation*," Johnnie added. "Are you really expecting your starchy strait-laced relatives who disapprove of you to accept this lovely girl who will turn the head of every man who looks at her?"

"It is certainly a problem," the Duke answered, "and you are neither of you being very helpful. But it was a mistake that Josina should have arrived here at this particular weekend."

"I thought that myself," Harry agreed, "and you may be certain of one thing, if Yvonne thinks that you are the slightest bit interested in her, she will scratch her eyes out!"

The Duke did not answer.

He thought angrily that, if there was one thing he disliked, it was people discussing his private affairs.

He walked out of the breakfast room, shutting the door loudly behind him.

Harry looked at Johnnie.

"I suppose I have put my foot in it," he said, "but you know as well as I do that the girl is a beauty and she will certainly need a very efficient chaperone."

"Rollo had better hurry and find someone to play the part, otherwise it may be too late," Johnnie replied.

"If you are looking that way yourself," Harry remarked, "there is no doubt that Kitty will have something to say about it."

*

Josina had then gone running upstairs and found to her relief that Mrs. Meadows was just coming along the corridor.

"Please, please – Mrs. Meadows," she asked as she reached her, "can you find me a habit to ride in. His Grace is going riding and you know – I have no riding habit with me."

"Great minds think alike," Mrs. Meadows replied, "because when I woke this mornin', I had the feelin' that His Grace would be askin' you to ride with him and I've got the very thing."

She paused, smiled and then continued,

"It was made for your mother when she was gettin' her trousseau ready to marry His Serene Highness."

"I would love to wear something of Mama's," Josina cried.

"What I always say about ridin' outfits is that the fashions don't change like gowns," Mrs. Meadows went on. "But I was thinkin' I had some more gowns upstairs, some that your mother never even wore and it might be possible to alter them. Perhaps when you've got the time you could try them on and we'll ask the seamstress to see what she can do."

"Oh, Mrs. Meadows, you are kind," Josina said. "Now, if I can have the habit, I shall have to hurry because His Grace said I was not to keep him waiting."

She walked into her bedroom and by the time she had taken off her gown Mrs. Meadows had brought in the habit that had been made for her mother.

It was plain and cut by the best tailor in London and it fitted almost as if it had been made specifically for her.

When she had put it on and looked at herself in the mirror, she thought that her mother would have been pleased.

At least one item in her trousseau had been of use even after all these years.

"You looks so much like your dear mother it gives me quite a turn," Mrs. Meadows was saying, "and it's a real pity she can't be here with you."

"I think she would love to have seen her old – home just once before she – died," Josina replied, "but you know it was – impossible."

"Well, you're here and that's what's important now, Miss Josina," Mrs. Meadows replied. "Now hurry downstairs or His Grace'll be champin' at the bit, as they says about the horses."

Josina laughed and it was a very happy sound.

As she ran downstairs just as Harry and Johnnie were walking towards the front door, she was thinking how perfect everything was.

And how lucky she was to have come to her mother's home.

This was what Nevon Hall was already beginning to mean to her.

CHAPTER FOUR

Josina found the Duke in the stables and he then proceeded to show her a number of horses.

They were all, she knew, not only well bred but exceptionally fine.

They went from stall to stall and while they were doing so, were joined by Johnnie and Harry.

"Are we allowed a choice?" Johnnie enquired.

"Of course," the Duke nodded, "except for the one I intend to ride myself and the one I have already chosen for Josina."

"I knew I would have to travel 'Second Class'!" Johnnie joked.

It would have been impossible to discard any horse in the Duke's stables without knowing that they would be considered superlative wherever they appeared.

Josina was thrilled with the stallion that he had chosen for her, which was all black except for a white star on its forehead.

She had no idea that the Duke had done it deliberately believing that the contrast between the animal's white star and her golden hair would be sensational.

As they rode off, Josina was not thinking of herself but of her mount, which was named 'Jet'.

She was hoping that she would not disgrace herself because it was a long time since she had been on a horse and then it had been only those that had come from livery stables.

The Duke led them down the drive and then cut off into a copse of silver birches onto a piece of flat land.

"This is where you ought to build your Racecourse, Rollo," Harry suggested.

"I have already thought of that," the Duke replied, "and I am having the plans drawn up."

Listening, Josina hoped that she would have a chance of riding over the course and that the Duke would not forget to invite her to come and stay once she had left The Hall.

She could not, however, help thinking that it was unlikely.

Why should he bother himself with a young, rather boring relation when he could fill the house with glamorous and exotic women like the Comtesse.

Then, because she was riding again, she forgot everything but the joy of galloping faster than she had ever galloped before in her life.

Later on she managed to jump several tall hedges without falling off.

When they were on their way back to The Hall, the Duke turned t0 Josina and said,

"I must congratulate you, Josina. I had always been told that your mother was an excellent horsewoman and now I can see that you have inherited that great talent from her."

"And from my father," Josina replied. "He was an outstanding rider, but he could only afford the sort of horses he really enjoyed when he had a lucky break."

She spoke without thinking and then she mused that it was a mistake to keep referring to her father's passion for gambling. It was certainly a subject that she must not mention when she met her other relations.

They rode back to the stables.

Having dismounted, Josina patted Jet and said to the Duke,

"Thank you, thank you. I have never enjoyed myself more and even if I am so stiff that I can hardly walk it will have been worth it!"

"You must talk to Mrs. Meadows," the Duke smiled. "She has a cure for stiffness, which she recommends to my friends. It contains, I believe, herbs that come from the Herb Garden here at Nevon Hall."

"Oh, Mama did tell me about the herbs," Josina replied excitedly. "And the garden is something I must see – before I leave."

"Are you in such a hurry to go?" the Duke enquired.

"No – *no* – of course not," Josina replied, "but I realise that I am upsetting the numbers of your house party – and for that I should apologise."

The Duke did not answer, but she thought as they walked towards the house that he looked at her in a strange way, as if she worried him for some reason.

'What I ought to have done,' she told herself as she went up the steps to the front door, 'was to have written to him after Mama died and explained why I had to come to England.'

Then she remembered that her mother had begged her to leave at once.

She thought that perhaps she had been afraid that the Duke would have then been given the opportunity to refuse to take her in.

If he had done so, she would have had nowhere to go and no money.

'Mama was wise in making me promise to leave immediately,' Josina thought. 'At the same time it is embarrassing and I must try to be very tactful about it.'

She went up the stairs to her bedroom and found Mrs. Meadows waiting for her.

"I'm sure you've enjoyed yourself, Miss Josina," the housekeeper remarked.

"It has been wonderful," Josina enthused. "I have never ridden such a magnificent stallion before, but I know – I am going to be stiff and His Grace tells me that you have a special remedy for it."

"It be a herbal remedy and I've put it in the bath I've already had prepared for you," Mrs. Meadows answered.

"It's very kind of you," Josina smiled.

She had taken off her riding hat as she was speaking and Mrs. Meadows took it from her.

She was putting it on a shelf inside the wardrobe when the door opened and the Comtesse came in.

Josina looked round in surprise and she said,

"I am given to understand that you have been riding with the Duke and the other two gentlemen of the party. Surely you have enough sense to know you should have had a chaperone with you?"

Josina stared at her in surprise and the Comtesse carried on,

"You are a *jeune fille* not a married woman and in England you should behave properly and with utmost discretion."

There was a hardness in her broken accent and Josina, feeling embarrassed and uncomfortable, stammered,

"I-I am sorry – if I have done – anything – wrong."

"You come here uninvited," the Comtesse went on, "and you should keep your place. Let me tell you that in England young women are seen and not heard!"

"I am – sorry," Josina apologised again, "but His Grace asked me to go – riding and it was – something I was very anxious – to do."

"I am sure you were," the Comtesse said in a nasty tone. "But you are pushing yourself at His Grace simply because you are a relative. You should be aware, however, that men find *debutantes* a bore, in point of fact usually they have as little to do with them as possible."

As she finished speaking, Mrs. Meadows, who had been hidden by the open door of the wardrobe, came further into the room.

The Comtesse looked at her in surprise and then finished,

"I have warned you and the best thing you can do is to keep yourself to yourself, as long as you are in this house."

She flounced round as she stopped speaking and, walking from the room, closed the door sharply behind her.

Josina stood looking after her in consternation.

It had never occurred to her for a moment that she should not have gone riding when the Duke invited her to.

Anyway she had not been aware until she reached the stables that none of the other three women in the party intended to accompany them.

Mrs. Meadows came to her side and said quietly,

"Now don't you go worryin' yourself, Miss Josina, at what that Madame la Comtesse has been sayin' to you. She's only jealous because His Grace has been payin' you a little attention."

"J-jealous?" Josina enquired in surprise.

"I'm afraid you'll find there's many a lady as will behave like her where His Grace is concerned."

"You mean – they don't like anybody else – to talk to him?" Josina asked.

Mrs. Meadows gave a little laugh.

"What they minds is His Grace lookin' at anybody else but them!"

"I-I don't – want to be a – nuisance," Josina admitted.

"You're not a nuisance to anybody else," Mrs. Meadows replied soothingly, "and, if you wants my opinion, she's a nasty piece of work as shouldn't be in this house in the first place!"

Josina looked at Mrs. Meadows in bewilderment and Mrs. Meadows battled on,

"Her lady's maid's been tellin' us what Madame gets up to in London, like havin' duels fought over her."

"Duels?" Josina repeated, "But I thought that duels were now forbidden to take place in England."

"They happens just the same with gentlemen as has no other way of settlin' their grievances," Mrs. Meadows answered, "and the Comte, so I hears, be a very jealous man and resents the way that Madame carries on when he's not there."

"So he fights – duels!" Josina said slowly.

She was thinking as she spoke that it was a duel that had killed her father.

He, however, had duelled with a man who had accused him of cheating, which she knew was something that he would never have stooped to.

He had intended to teach the man a lesson but instead his accuser, who was an Italian, had fired before the count of ten. And D'Arcy Marsh had died in consequence.

Without saying anything further Josina undressed and climbed into the delightfully hot bath.

It was fragrant with the scent of herbs and flowers and she could feel the warm water soaking away the stiffness that she already felt attacking in her limbs.

Although she said nothing, Mrs. Meadows went on talking.

"It's always the same," she said, "where there's a handsome man, especially if he's a Duke! Women buzz round him like bees round a honeypot and if they sees another woman so much as lookin' in his direction, they becomes wasps and stings!"

Because it sounded so funny, Josina gave a little laugh.

"I'm just tellin' you not to worry your pretty head about it," Mrs. Meadows asserted, "and I'm sure when the party's over on Monday, His Grace will take you to stay with one of his relations,"

Josina could not help feeling even more depressed by this prospect.

She clearly remembered her father telling her how strait-laced the Nevon relations were and it was impossible for her to forget that none of them had ever spoken to her mother again once she had run away.

If they only knew how happy she had been, Josina thought, perhaps they would have forgiven her.

She gave a little shiver because they had not forgiven Lady Margaret for refusing to become a

Princess and they were not very likely in the circumstances to accept the daughter of a marriage that in their eyes should never have taken place.

'Perhaps I should try to earn my living somehow,' Josina reflected to herself.

She wondered what she could do and how it would be possible for her to make any money.

As her bath was carried out by the housemaids, Mrs. Meadows helped her into a pretty gown, which she told her had belonged to her mother.

It was slightly old-fashioned but not black and Josina wondered if anyone would think it strange that she was wearing pale blue muslin.

Then she told herself that if, as the Duke had said, his relations disapproved of him, they were not likely to be present at the Steeplechase.

Even if they were, they would not know who she was.

As she went down the stairs to the drawing room, she was afraid that the Comtesse might be there, remonstrating with the Duke as well as having been unpleasant to her.

She knew, however, as she entered the room and the Duke smiled at her, that he was not aware of what had occurred upstairs.

He put a glass of champagne into her hand and said,

"I think you deserve this. Has Mrs. Meadows taken away all the unpleasant after-effects of what was an enchanting morning?"

"That is exactly the right word for it," Josina added. "For me it was enchanting and I shall always remember the first stallion I rode in England – and how exciting it was!"

The Duke grinned and was just about to reply when the Comtesse slipped her arm through his.

"There is something I want to tell you, Rollo," she said in her seductive voice.

Because Josina knew that it was expected of her, she moved away.

As she did so, she was conscious that Kitty was talking animatedly with Johnnie.

Doris was looking up at Harry in a provocative manner from under her mascaraed eyelashes.

They had an early luncheon, which was light and delicious.

As soon as it was over, the ladies all climbed into a carriage that was to carry them to where the Steeplechase was to be held.

The men set off ahead of them on the horses they were to ride.

Josina was quite certain that the Duke would be the winner and she had realised this morning what a sublime rider he was and knew that her mother would have been proud of him.

It was a family tradition that all its members were good equestrians.

Josina had heard her mother laugh at the antics of some riders they watched in the various places where they had stayed.

Josina had been aware instantly that the Duke seemed to be a part of his horse and that both Harry and Johnnie were also excellent riders.

They then reached the nearby estate where the Steeplechase was to take place. It was in the opposite direction from where they had ridden this morning.

Josina could see that everything had been laid out and already there was a growing crowd of spectators.

This increased immediately they arrived as carriage-loads of people came from neighbouring houses.

There were also farmers driving wagons and a number of women arrived in donkey carts.

Josina soon realised that the course was a complicated one over three miles in length and it twisted and turned in sight of those watching for the first mile.

They also had an excellent view of the Winning Post.

All the while they were being driven to the course the Comtesse was talking animatedly to the other two ladies completely ignoring Josina.

She had felt embarrassed during luncheon whenever the Duke spoke to her, remembering how the Comtesse had cautioned her.

She had known without even looking at the French woman that her eyes were flashing fire and there was an expression on her face of anger and dislike.

'She wants to spoil everything,' Josina thought.

It was uncomfortable to sit opposite her in the carriage and so Josina climbed out and walked towards the starting line.

As she approached some men on horseback, they raised their hats.

"I suppose," one asked, "as you are staying at The Hall you will be backing the Duke, but I should be grateful if you could wish me into second place."

"I will certainly try," Josina answered him.

She thought that these men were being friendly, which was something she needed at the moment.

She had no idea that the man who had spoken to her and the others seeing her for the first time were thinking how lovely she was.

They were muttering to themselves that it was just the Duke's luck to have such an attractive young woman in his party.

In fact two other men had already gone up to the Duke to ask who she was.

"A new face, Rollo," one of them exclaimed. "I cannot imagine how you manage to find them. I have not seen anyone so pretty for a long time."

"I was just about to say the same thing," the man beside him added. "Who is she? Surely you don't intend to keep her entirely to yourself?"

The Duke, realising the sensation that Josina was causing amongst his guests, rode up to where she was standing.

"You will see better, Josina, if you watch from the carriage," he said. "Tell the coachman to let you sit up on the box. You will have a much better view from there than from inside."

Josina smiled at him gratefully.

She was certain that he had realised she had left the carriage because she had not liked being cooped up with the other women who obviously resented her.

"I would indeed like to sit on the box," she said to the Duke. "Thank you for suggesting it."

"We will be off in a few minutes," the Duke informed her, "so you had better get up to your vantage point right away."

She obeyed him.

As she watched the start of the race, she was praying that the Duke would be the winner.

She felt certain, however, that it was a foregone conclusion.

He won, but only by a length, and Harry to his great delight came in second.

There were prizes, which were presented by the Duke and, when they eventually returned to the house, it was too late for tea.

There was instead champagne waiting for them as well as some delicious *pâté* sandwiches and *petits fours*, which were almost as good as those that Josina had enjoyed in France.

A number of neighbours had been asked to The Hall by the Duke,

Because Josina thought tactfully that it would be a mistake for them to enquire as to who she was, she slipped away.

She went to the library to find some books to read, but the Curator had already gone home.

She browsed among the bookshelves, eventually finding several books on England that looked as if they might be fascinating.

She was carrying two of them in her arms when the library door opened and the Duke came in.

"I had a feeling that I might find you here," he began. "I thought I should tell you that dinner will be late this evening after my friends have gone, so there is no need for you to hurry."

"I was just going upstairs with these books," Josina said.

"As we are alone," the Duke added, "I have a chance to talk to you about yourself, which has not been possible to do before."

Because she knew that this was what he expected, Josina sat down on a sofa by the fireplace.

"I have been thinking it over," the Duke went on, "and I have decided that it would be a mistake to take you immediately to one of our Nevon relatives."

Josina looked surprised and a little apprehensive.

"Y-you mean," she responded after a moment, "that you don't – think they will – want me?"

"I think it would be wise," the Duke said quietly, "for them first to hear about you and realise how charming you are and very different from what they might have anticipated before you actually meet them."

Josina clasped her hands together.

She wondered if she should suggest that it would be best if she went abroad.

But she knew that would be impossible, as she had no money.

She thought miserably how tiresome it must be for the Duke to be confronted with an unwanted relative.

"What I have decided," he was now saying, "is that I will take you to meet my Godmother, Lady Swinton."

Josina did not speak and he continued,

"She has been a wonderful friend to me and, as my mother died when I was young, I have always thought of her as my 'second mother'."

Josina was listening intently as he carried on,

"She is over sixty now, but she is still very active, and very influential in the Social world. I know if I ask her she will look after you, she will do it for me and what is more, enjoy doing it."

"Are you – are you quite – sure of that?" Josina asked hesitatingly.

"I am absolutely certain," the Duke answered, "and that is why I am going to take you on Monday to Lady Swinton. I know you will be very happy with her."

He paused before he went on,

"I have thought it over very carefully. I know she will introduce you to her friends, then to our relations and they will have a very different picture of you than they might have expected otherwise."

"It is very – very kind of – you to take – so much trouble," Josina said. "I was – wondering today how I could – earn my living and not be an – encumbrance to you, but I am afraid I have very – few talents that could earn me money."

"You are not to think of such a thing," the Duke replied. "Your mother entrusted you to my care and I intend to look after you. I will give you an allowance so that you can buy what clothes you need, for any gifts you give to Lady Swinton and tips for her servants."

"Thank – you," Josina murmured.

She did indeed feel very grateful.

At the same time the fact that he was being so generous made her feel shy.

'If only Papa could have died when he was on a winning streak,' she thought, 'I would not have to be obliged to the Duke so that I cannot spend anything without asking him first.'

As if he sensed what she was thinking, the Duke said,

"You are not to worry or think that you are imposing on me. I assure you I have a long list of relations, some of whom I have never seen, who expect me to support them and who each receive an annual allowance of quite a considerable sum."

He gave a short laugh before he added,

"I am only exceedingly grateful to my predecessors for being rich so that I can do things I never dreamt of doing before I came into the title."

"I want to say – 'thank you' to you for – being so – kind to me," Josina stammered, "but there are – not enough words in the – English language."

It flashed through her mind as she spoke that there were more in French.

She wondered whether he gave presents to the Comtesse and if she thanked him very eloquently in her own language.

"Then that is settled," the Duke said, "and now, Josina, I want you to enjoy yourself in England and be happy. You are very beautiful and you will find that there are a great many men who will pursue you, flatter you and doubtless ask you for your hand in marriage."

He spoke lightly, as if to make it sound amusing, but Josina replied to him seriously,

"I will – never marry – anybody unless I – love him in the – same way that Mama and Papa – loved each other."

She was silent for a moment before she resumed,

"Our relations may think it was – wrong, but as Papa once said – no one can resist *real* love."

"I am sure he was right," the Duke agreed, "and now, while you go and dress for dinner, I will say 'goodbye' to my friends."

He walked to the door before he turned and added,

"Incidentally there will be several charming young men coming to dinner, so you will not be bored by the same faces and the same conversation that you have heard before."

"Of course I have not – been bored," Josina cried. "It has been very – exciting listening to what – you have been talking about – and to be in such – a beautiful house."

She looked around as she spoke and added,

"This is such a vast and interesting library."

"I thought you would appreciate it," the Duke answered. "I realise that while you have travelled a great deal for a young woman, you have also travelled in your mind."

"That is what – Mama said I had to do," Josina said, "especially because I had very few people to talk to."

The Duke looked surprised and she went on,

"When Papa went to the casinos, Mama and I stayed at home and, because we were continually moving from one place to another, we did not make many friends. In fact Papa considered that most of the people he knew were unsuitable to bring home."

The Duke thought for a moment before he said,

"Are you telling me that your mother did not go to parties or balls or take part in any of the festivities, which I always understood were very much a part of the places where your father gambled?"

"That is right," Josina agreed. "Papa gambled at the tables, and then he came home. He always wanted to be with Mama, so we spent most of the day planning an exciting dinner for him with just the three of us present."

The Duke sighed.

"I have a feeling that people are going to find that hard to believe. Our relatives have, of course, heard about the gambling casinos at Monte Carlo, Marienbad and Baden-Baden. They always imagined your father and mother enjoying the gaieties of the Fancy Dress balls and the supper parties where a woman would dance on the tables."

He appeared to be talking to himself, but Josina stared at him in astonishment.

"If that sort of thing went on, I never heard about it," she said. "Anyway Papa was only concerned with gambling, which he enjoyed. When he was not playing, he came home to Mama."

"So what did you and your mother do while you were waiting for him?" the Duke asked her.

"We went for walks, we visited the Museums, the Churches and, of course, anything that was of historical interest in the neighbourhood. Our only difficulty was to find the books we wanted to read. Because we moved from place to place, it was not practicable to buy them because they weighed down our luggage."

"I believe you," the Duke said, "but I think it will be very difficult for our relatives to do the same."

"I am telling you the truth," Josina cried, "and – please – I don't want to be with relatives who are going to be – unkind and disagreeable about – Papa."

"I understand your feelings," the Duke said, "and that is exactly why I am taking you to Lady Swinton. She will understand, as no one else will, the difficulties about coming back to England and taking your rightful place, and I mean this, your *rightful* place, as a member of the Nevon family."

Josina rose to her feet.

With her fingers clasped together she went nearer to the Duke.

"You are quite – quite certain that you would not prefer me to – go away? Perhaps if you gave me a little money – just enough to live on – I could find a quiet village somewhere where – no one will be interested in me – and I could find – something to do – perhaps teach the village children – or something like that."

With her face turned up to his the Duke thought it would be impossible for her to hide herself away.

Wherever she went, the men, whatever their age, would be bowled over by her beauty.

"I have decided what I am going to do about you, Josina," he said. "I think it is for the best and is exactly what I want to do."

"Then, of course, I will – do it," Josina answered, "and – thank you – thank you again for being so kind – I know how grateful – Mama would have been."

There was a little sob in her voice as she spoke about her mother.

Then, because she thought that the Duke might think that she was being over-dramatic, she turned and ran from the library.

She just remembered to pick up the books that she had chosen as she went.

As the door closed behind her, the Duke stood for a long time in front of the fireplace, a frown between his eyes.

CHAPTER FIVE

The dinner party, which consisted of a number of young men and only one extra woman, was very amusing.

Josina was feeling particularly happy because Mrs. Meadows had brought her a very pretty evening gown to wear.

"It's one of her Ladyship's as she had for her trousseau," she explained, "but in them days it was a crinoline."

Josina looked at it somewhat anxiously, but Mrs. Meadows went on,

"The seamstress is very skilful with her needle and she's drawn back the skirt so that it's now a fashionable bustle."

Josina, seeing how it had been altered, gave an exclamation of delight.

"How clever," she enthused, "and it is such a pretty colour."

"I just knew it would suit you, Miss Josina," Mrs. Meadows replied. "Your mother, bless her heart, would have looked ever so lovely in it."

"Did she take nothing with her – when she ran away?" Josina enquired.

"Only a very few things. We all thought it was a cryin' shame that she never wore her lovely gowns. They were all put up in the attics and left there on His Grace's orders."

That, Josina thought, was very much to her advantage.

The gown, which was a pale green, made her, when she had it on, look like a nymph from the woods.

The skirt was draped at the front in Grecian fashion and the bodice accentuated her tiny waist. With the small bustle at the back Josina felt that she could compete with the other ladies in the party, even though there were only a few of them.

It was certainly new and exciting to find herself being complimented by the newcomers.

The Duke, however, was aware that they were too fulsome and too familiar to be accorded to a *debutante*.

The wine glasses were being constantly filled and, as the meal progressed, voices grew louder and the laughter more frequent.

. When the dinner was over, the ladies left the dining room and the Comtesse remarked in a spiteful manner to Josina,

"Where can you possibly have found yourself such an elegant gown? Is it not true that you have come here straight from a Convent?"

It was quite obvious that she did not believe the story, but Josina replied politely,

"This gown belonged to my mother and it has been altered to fit me."

The Comtesse then gave her an unpleasant look and turned away to speak to one of the other ladies.

Because she had made her feel uneasy, Josina crossed the room to look out of the window.

The moon was rising over the trees in the Park and the first stars were beginning to appear in the sky.

It occurred to her that she had still seen only a little of the family house and the grounds.

And if the Duke was taking her to London on Monday, as he had suggested, she might never come back to Nevon Hall.

'I have just tomorrow to see everything I can,' she told herself. 'I know that is what Mama would have wished me to do.'

The guests who had come in from the neighbourhood did not stay late.

In fact the Duke almost sent them away saying that they would all be tired after the Steeplechase.

As soon as the first guests started to say 'goodnight', Josina slipped away upstairs to her bedroom.

Two men had already told her that they wished to see her again and tried to make an assignation in the woods when she went riding.

They even suggested coming to The Hall, but she felt that this would only annoy the Duke and she was sure that the Comtesse would be very rude about the idea.

It was therefore wiser, she decided, just to disappear.

She undressed slowly, not ringing for the maid who had told her that she would come if she wanted her.

She then sat in front of the mirror on the dressing table, brushing her hair as her mother had always told her she should do.

"You have such beautiful hair, my dearest," she had said, "and, as it is very long, you must remember to brush it every night and never let it look untidy or neglected."

It was now that Josina realised guiltily that she had not paid any attention to her appearance since her mother had died.

Her hair had therefore been neglected.

'I must certainly make it look right when I go to London,' she determined.

She felt a little shiver of fear go through her at what might be waiting for her there.

'Even if the Duke's Godmother is kind to me,' she told herself, 'our relations will now learn of my arrival in England.'

They would undoubtedly be extremely critical and perhaps disagreeable, but there was, however, she told herself sensibly, nothing she could do about it.

She must just face every difficulty as and when it occurred.

When she had finished brushing her hair, she climbed into bed, but she did not draw the curtains.

Instead she lay gazing at the stars that came out in a dazzling profusion in front of her.

Quite suddenly she decided that it would be a great mistake for her not to see the beauty of the garden by moonlight.

She thought that by now all the guests would have gone to bed and would be sleeping soundly.

She had heard their voices as they had come up the stairs and the Comtesse saying 'goodnight' as she passed her room on the way to where she was sleeping.

It now occurred to Josina that the Comtesse's room was near the Master suite, which was at the end of the corridor.

She had seen her emerging from it when they went down to luncheon and she had drawn back quickly into her room so that they did not have to go downstairs together.

Mrs. Meadows had told her about the Master suite and how many Dukes had slept there over the centuries.

"I'll show it to you tomorrow, Miss Josina," she promised, "and you'll see a portrait of your grandmother in the boudoir that adjoins it."

"I would really love to see it," Josina had replied. "Mama often talked about her."

"Well, there's quite a number of your ancestors in that room," Mrs. Meadows went on, "includin' one of your great-grandfather, who was a much admired dandy in the reign of King George IV."

Josina then knew that she could not leave The Hall until she had seen it.

There was indeed so much to see and so little time left in which to enjoy it all.

On an impulse she jumped out of bed.

Putting on the woollen dressing gown that she had worn at the Convent, she cautiously opened her bedroom door.

As she expected, most of the candles in their silver sconces that lit the corridor had been extinguished. Only in every third sconce was a candle left burning to last through the night.

Everything was very quiet, but she was that aware there would be a night porter on duty in the hall and he would doubtless be fast asleep in the big padded and hooded chair near the front door.

She therefore tiptoed her way across the top of the stairs to where she knew that there was another staircase. This had only two lights, but they were enough for her to see her way down to the ground floor.

She recognised that she could not leave the house by the front, but was aware that there was a garden door just beyond one of the sitting rooms.

It was locked and bolted top and bottom, but it was not difficult for her to draw back the bolts and open it.

Then she was in the garden at the back of the house and the moonlight made it an enchanted Fairyland.

There was the fountain playing in the centre of the green lawn and beyond it there was a bowling green.

Then a towering cascade, which ran down from the shrubbery, twisting its way eventually to the lake.

Behind the cascade Josina knew was the Herb Garden that she so much wanted to visit.

But she thought that she must leave that until daylight.

In the meantime she was thrilled by the beauty of the moonlight shimmering on the shrubs and the flowerbeds. And it turned the fountain into a cascade of flickering lights.

The water, as it fell back into the sculpted stone basin, looked like a thousand tiny rainbows.

Josina thought nothing in the world could be more beautiful or more romantic.

She could picture her mother gazing at the fountain and dreaming of the man she loved.

Perhaps it was here that she had admitted that love was irresistible and a rapture that she could not reject or refuse.

'Of course Mama had to run away,' Josina told herself, 'but the beauty of all this was always irreversible in her mind.'

She remembered how when they were in dingy uncomfortable lodgings her mother would seem to be miles away.

There would be a wistful expression in her eyes, which Josina thought that she now understood.

'She was thinking lovingly of her home and the beauty of it,' she told herself.

She went closer to the fountain and stood with her hands on the stone basin.

She was watching the water being thrown up so that it seemed almost to touch the stars.

Then it fell back into the basin, cascading over the water lilies beneath.

She was so entranced that she stood watching it for a long time even though there was a great deal more that she wanted to explore.

As she turned away from the fountain, she was suddenly very still.

She was aware that, while she had been watching the fountain, a man had appeared around the corner of the house.

She wondered if perhaps it was the Duke or maybe one of the other gentlemen.

Then, as two other men joined him, they went towards one of the windows and appeared to be doing something to it.

It seemed to Josina so strange that she stood there watching them.

Why were they so interested in this particular window on this side of The Hall?

Even at this distance she could see that they were not the Duke or any of the other gentlemen.

She now became aware that they were all bending forward to touch the window.

It was as if they were trying either to prevent the glass from falling or making sure that it did not crash to the ground.

It was then she remembered something that Mrs. Meadows had told her.

The Comte de Soissons was so jealous of his wife that he had already fought two duels over her.

And his opponent in one of them had been fatally wounded.

'A duel!'

Josina felt as if the words were being screamed at her.

It was a duel that had killed her father and, if the Duke took part in one, he too might be killed.

She could imagine nothing more horrible or ignominious than the Duke of Nevondale, who was of such importance, losing his life over a woman like the Comtesse.

There would be a scandal, during which terrible things would be said and whispered about the Duke all over the country.

Also there would be sneers and gibes about the woman who had seduced him into such a predicament.

Now Josina saw that the men working on the window had succeeded in what they were attempting to achieve.

They were pushing the window up and one man was already in the act of climbing over the windowsill.

She must save the Duke!

And also the illustrious family name from being dragged through the mud.

It was almost as if her mother was commanding her to do so!

Making for the bushes on one side of the garden, Josina reached the shelter of them and she reckoned that the men would be too occupied with entering the house to notice her.

She found a path that led directly towards The Hall and started to run faster than she had ever run before.

By the time she reached the end of the path and looked apprehensively through the bushes, there was no sign of the three men.

The door that she had left The Hall by was not far away.

She reached it and tore up the secondary staircase and then along the corridor.

She went first to the Comtesse's bedroom and opened the door abruptly without knocking.

As she entered, she saw that there were candles burning on the dressing table and beside the bed – which was empty!

She knew then with a little throb of her heart where the Comtesse would be found.

Even as she moved back into the corridor, she thought that she heard footsteps in the distance.

It might be her imagination, but because she was frightened of being seen, she ran not to the Master suite, but to an open door that was almost opposite.

As she went inside the room, she realised that it was the boudoir that Mrs. Meadows had spoken to her about.

The curtains were not pulled over the windows and the moonlight shone on the elegant furniture and the pictures she so longed to see.

There was a door to the left of her and she thought that it must be a communicating door leading into the Master suite.

She pulled it open and by the light of two candles burning by the bedside she could see that there were two people lying in the huge bed.

They were not asleep but talking to each other.

Although Josina could not hear what was said, she could easily recognise the Comtesse's rather shrill voice and from the sound of it she knew that she was angry.

She stood still.

Then the Duke saw her and exclaimed in astonishment,

"Josina! What are you doing here?"

Because she was so breathless Josina's voice sounded strange even to herself as she answered him,

"The Comte – I think it is – the Comte – who is – c-coming up – the stairs – with two – men – to fight you in – a – *duel*."

Both the Duke and the Comtesse sat up to look at her and she could see the surprise and consternation on their faces.

The Comtesse then gave a little cry.

"My – husband! It cannot – be true!"

Even as she spoke, her voice no more than a whisper, the handle of the door that opened into the corridor turned.

Then there was a sharp knock.

"Open this door," a man's voice ordered, "or I will break it down!"

The Duke sprang out of bed and as he did so he said to the Comtesse,

"Get under the bed!"

She threw back the bedclothes and obeyed him.

As she crawled under the valance, the Duke picked up his robe that had been thrown over a chair and put it on.

The knock on the door came again more loudly.

"Open this door or, as I have just said, I will break it down!"

There was no doubt that the man speaking had a pronounced French accent.

The Duke then walked towards the door and as he did so the Comtesse disappeared.

The Duke glanced quickly round to make that sure she was well hidden from sight.

Then he said in a sleepy voice,

"What is all this about?"

"Open this door, I tell you!" the Comte shouted.

The Duke put his hand out to turn the key and unlock the door.

Josina was suddenly aware that, if the Comte entered, he would think it strange that she was standing in the doorway that led to the boudoir.

He might even guess that she had come to warn the Duke of his approach.

In which case he would begin a search for his wife and find her hiding under the bed.

Hardly thinking of the consequence, but acting impulsively, she rushed to where the Comtesse had pulled back the bedclothes and slipped into the bed.

Even as she did so, the Duke unlocked the door and the Comte burst in.

"*De Soissons!*" the Duke exclaimed in well-simulated surprise. "What on earth are you doing here at this hour?"

"I am looking for my wife," the Comte replied grimly, "and I understand – "

His voice stopped suddenly.

He had looked towards the bed and saw Josina's golden hair spread over the pillows.

For a moment he seemed turned to stone, as if he could not believe his own eyes.

Then he turned to the Duke and said in a very different tone of voice,

"I must apologise, Your Grace. I was told on good authority that my wife was with you, but I can see that I was mistaken. Pardon me. I can only offer you my most sincere apologies for having entered your house in such a manner."

The Duke drew himself up so that he seemed immensely taller than the small Frenchman.

"I think, *Monsieur le Comte*," he said slowly, "this is an incident that should be immediately forgotten. I can only ask you to withdraw in the same way that you entered my house and as quickly as possible."

"Of course, of course," the Comte agreed.

He then stared at Josina again as if he thought that she could not be real.

Then with a bow, such as only a Frenchman can make, he said to the Duke,

"Forgive me, Your Grace. I am humiliated and embarrassed that I should have insulted you in this way."

The Duke did not reply.

As the Comte turned to go, he merely closed the bedroom door behind him and locked it again.

He did not move away from the door.

Josina guessed that he was listening to make quite certain that the Frenchman and his attendants had left and would not search any further.

The Comtesse would then emerge from under the bed and it would be extremely embarrassing.

Without speaking Josina slipped from beneath the bedclothes.

Reaching the communicating door into the boudoir, she went through it without looking back.

She crossed the moonlit room slowly and, as she passed through the other door, she was aware that the Comte and the men with him had reached the hall.

They were telling the footman, who was staring at them in astonishment, to open the front door.

Josina ran across the corridor and into her own room.

Only then did she realise how shocked she felt at finding the Comtesse in bed with the Duke.

Somehow, although she could see that the Frenchwoman was flirting with him, she had not expected the Duke to take another man's wife into his bed.

Of course she had heard in Paris and other parts of the world of men and women having *affaires de*

Coeur, but in her innocence she had not been aware of the full implications of what that meant.

The Comtesse's possessive jealousy of the Duke was because he was her lover.

'How stupid of me not to realise that,' Josina chided herself.

At the same time, however reprehensible it was, she had done the right thing in saving the Head of her mother's family from a vulgar scandal.

Also from fighting a duel when he might have been injured or worse killed like her father had been

'I saved – him! *I saved – him*!' she told herself as she snuggled down in her bed.

He might be behaving what the world would call badly, but she knew that he was a kind man as well as being a very impressive one.

She thought of how well he rode and how distinguished he looked at the head of the table.

Whatever people might think about him, in this beautiful house he seemed perfectly fitted to follow in the footsteps of his Nevon ancestors, who had been an integral part of the history of England.

'How could I allow him, Mama, to be criticised and condemned?'

As she fell asleep, she had the distinct idea that her mother was pleased with her.

*

Josina awoke because the maid was moving about in her bedroom.

She thought that it must be early and perhaps the Duke wanted her to go riding with him again.

Opening her eyes, she sat up in bed.

"What is the time, Emily?" she asked.

"It's nearly seven o'clock, miss," the maid answered, "and His Grace says will you be dressed and ready to go to London by half-past ten. I've brought your breakfast and His Grace'll not want to be kept waitin'."

"Going to London?" Josina exclaimed in astonishment.

The maid put a tray with her breakfast on it in front of her and she started to eat hurriedly.

She could only think that the Duke had changed his mind about taking her to Lady Swinton on Monday and, because of what had happened last night, he was taking her there today.

'Perhaps he does not wish me to see the Comtesse again after last night,' she thought to herself.

But it seemed odd that he should be in such a hurry.

"What about Nanny?" she asked.

The maid had come back into the room with a can of hot water.

"His Grace says as Miss Tate is to follow with your luggage, miss, by train," Emily explained.

There seemed to be nothing that Josina could say to this and, when she had finished her breakfast, Emily helped her to dress.

She had only the black dress to wear with the coat and widow's bonnet that she had arrived in.

She realised that she must not waste time in talking to Emily and so keep the Duke waiting.

It was actually one minute to half-past ten when, carrying her handbag, Josina ran down the stairs.

To her surprise the Duke was already seated in a travelling chariot that was drawn by a team of four horses.

Because it had been built for swiftness, there was room only for two people in the front and behind, perched somewhat precariously, sat a groom.

The hood of the carriage was down and, as Josina climbed in beside the Duke, she was aware that it would be impossible to talk intimately with the groom so close behind them.

They drove off in silence.

As they trotted down the drive, Josina thought dismally that perhaps she would never see The Hall again.

With a pang she remembered too that she had not paid a visit to the Herb Garden.

As soon as they were outside the village on the high road, the Duke gave his team their heads.

They moved at a tremendous pace. It was so fast that Josina could never remember having travelled at such a speed before.

In a way it was fascinating.

At the same time she was vividly conscious that the Duke's lips were set in a tight line and his chin was very square.

'He is angry with me,' she thought suddenly.

She wanted to cry out that she had only done what she had to save him.

She could not understand why he should be angry.

It was obvious that he was taking her away to be with his Godmother because he no longer wanted her with him.

On and on they drove until after about two hours they stopped at a coaching inn.

"I expect you will want to wash the dust from your face and hands," the Duke said, speaking for the first time since they had left The Hall.

"I will send you up something to drink and give you exactly ten minutes before we continue our journey with a fresh team of horses."

He did not wait for her to reply, but stepped out on his side of the travelling chariot.

An ostler came to help Josina to the ground and, because she had no wish to make the Duke any angrier than he was already, she went upstairs.

A maid in a mobcap then brought her some hot water.

Soon afterwards a tray bearing a glass of champagne and some *pâté* sandwiches arrived.

They were exactly the same as she had eaten last night at Nevon Hall and she guessed that the Duke must have brought them with him rather than rely on what would be provided at a wayside inn.

The champagne revived Josina and she was certain that it too must have come with them from The Hall.

Because she was frightened she watched the clock and returned to the courtyard before the ten minutes was up.

As she expected, the horses had been changed and now there was a fresh team between the shafts.

The Duke was already in the driving seat and, as she joined him, he quizzed her,

"You are all right now?"

It was a question and Josina answered quickly,

"Yes, perfectly, thank you."

The Duke drove off and once again they were travelling at a tremendous speed.

It took them nearly five hours to reach London and Josina wondered why, if Nanny could have gone by train, they could not have done the same.

She supposed that the Duke had his own reasons and she wished that he would talk to her and not be so aloof.

As it happened, it would have been very difficult because of the speed that they were moving at.

Her father had often told her that, when a man was concentrating on either riding or driving, he did not want a woman chatting at him like a cockatoo.

The first buildings of London now came in sight.

Then they were going slower through the crowded streets until finally Josina guessed that they were in Park Lane.

Her mother had told her that this was where Nevon House was situated and it was from there that she had made her debut as a young girl.

The great house looked out over the trees in Hyde Park.

Because her mother had described it so vividly, Josina knew which house they were going to before the Duke stopped in front of it.

A red carpet had been rolled down over the steps and there was a butler waiting at the open door.

"Welcome back, Your Grace," he intoned bowing respectfully.

The Duke walked into the hall and handed his tall hat and gloves to a footman.

"There are refreshments in the study, Your Grace," the butler announced.

"Thank you, Dawson," the Duke replied. "But I feel sure that Miss Marsh would like to go upstairs."

"Mrs. Ward's waiting for her, Your Grace," the butler replied.

Josina walked up the stairs and found, as she expected, the housekeeper at the top of them.

She was younger than Mrs. Meadows, a woman of about forty and Josina thought it unlikely that she would remember her mother.

She took Josina into a very luxuriously furnished room and helped her take off her coat and hat.

She then offered to arrange her hair, which had become untidy from the speed that they had been travelling.

Finally, when she had washed, Mrs. Ward said,

"His Grace'll be waitin' for you, miss, in the study."

They had exchanged only a few words about the journey, but Josina was now feeling apprehensive.

As she went slowly down the stairs, she found herself praying,

'Please, God – let him be kind to me – please, God, don't – let him – be angry. Why, oh, why, must I go – away?'

She knew that she had no wish to meet his Godmother or anybody else from the family.

She wanted to stay with him because he was a relation of her mother's and because he had been kind to her since she had arrived at The Hall so unexpectedly.

As she went into the study, her eyes seemed to have filled her small face.

She thought that the Duke gazed at her for a long moment before he looked away again.

Then he said,

"I want you first to have a glass of champagne, Josina, and then listen to what I have to say to you."

"I-I am – listening," Josina answered him nervously.

The Duke gave her the champagne and there was then a pause as if he was trying to find the right words before he began,

"I expect you are wondering why I brought you away from The Hall so early and why we are here."

"I-I thought you were – angry with me," Josina replied.

She spoke in a very small voice that seemed to come jerkily from between her lips.

"Of course I am not angry with you," the Duke answered. "I am exceedingly grateful to you for rescuing me from what might have been a very unpleasant incident, in fact it was very clever of you. But how did you know that the Comte was in the house?"

"I-I was in the – garden," Josina explained, "and when I was standing by the fountain – I saw him and two other men starting to break in – through a window."

The Duke's lips tightened, but he did not speak as she went on,

"Mrs. Meadows – told me he had – killed a man in a – duel and I was frightened – because as it happened to – Papa – it might – happen to you."

"I can only say thank you," the Duke said, "but you do realise that in saving me you have compromised yourself?"

Josina looked at him in surprise.

It had never entered her mind that that was what she had done.

After what seemed a long time she asked,

"But surely – the Comtesse will not – speak of what – happened to – anyone?"

"We cannot be certain of that. It is the sort of story that would be repeated and repeated in all the

Clubs in London and would be greatly exaggerated as it went the rounds."

Now there was a harshness in his voice that was unmistakable and Josina enquired,

"Did you tell the Comtesse not to talk about it?"

"I forbade her to speak about it to anyone, either inside the house or out," the Duke replied, "but how can you be sure that you can trust a woman like her?"

Josina looked at him in astonishment.

There was no mistaking the scathing note in his voice.

But after all he must love the Comtesse, otherwise he would not have wanted to be with her and indeed in his bed.

Because Josina could think of nothing more to say at this point, there was silence until the Duke said,

"You must therefore realise, Josina, that in order to avoid any further unpleasantness, we must be married immediately."

Josina stared at him as if she could not believe what he had just said.

Then she whispered in a voice that he could hardly hear,

"M-married – did you say – *m-married?*"

CHAPTER SIX

There was an uncomfortable pause.

And then the Duke said,

"You must be aware that I cannot allow you to ruin your reputation before you have hardly set foot in England. You saved me and I am very grateful to you for that. At the same time we now have to be intelligent."

"I-I don't – understand," Josina murmured.

She felt as if the whole room was whirling around her and the whole world had turned topsy-turvy.

How could the Duke possibly mean that they were to be married?

How could she marry him when he loved the Comtesse!

"What I have thought out," the Duke was saying in what seemed a harsh voice, "is what I think is a very plausible story."

He hesitated for a moment as if he was trying to find the right words and then continued,

"I went abroad just after Christmas and what we are going to say is that we met, fell in love and married."

Josina gave a little gasp, but she did not interrupt.

"Unfortunately," he went on, "your mother was desperately ill and you felt that it was not only impossible for you to leave her but also people would think it strange that you could think of marrying me when you should be concentrating on your mother."

Josina thought that this at least sounded reasonable and the Duke carried on,

"I came back to England expecting that, as soon as your mother recovered, you would both come here when we would announce our marriage."

He made a gesture with his hand before he added,

"What happened is, of course, the truth. Your mother died unexpectedly and before she did so she insisted that you came immediately to me."

His voice seemed to deepen as he said in what Josina thought was a slightly embarrassed tone,

"You arrived at what we might call a somewhat unfortunate moment when I was giving a house party for my men friends and ladies who you would not have met in the ordinary way."

Josina was surprised.

She had not expected him to think, as she did, that the Comtesse was someone whom her mother would not have accepted.

"However," the Duke continued, "there was nothing I could do at that moment. Of course it would have been impossible for me to announce to my house party that we were married before my relations had been told."

He looked at Josina as if he expected her to agree. But because she was incapable of speech she merely slightly inclined her head.

"You do see," he resumed, "that the only thing we can do now is to be married by Special Licence. I will arrange for the Ceremony to take place very quietly, without anyone being aware of it, this evening at the Grosvenor Chapel, which is only a short distance from this house."

At last Josina found her voice.

"You are – quite certain – there is – nothing else we – can do?" she asked hesitatingly. "S-suppose I – just went back to Italy – and then you forgot all about me?"

"It would be impossible for my friends to forget you," the Duke answered, "and how could you possibly manage on your own without anyone to look after you?"

This, Josina knew, was indisputable.

She had never been alone and she could imagine nothing more frightening than arriving in Italy by herself.

She made a helpless little gesture with her hands and the Duke said,

"No, my solution is the only possible one and I do hope, Josina, that, when all this is past and done with, we can be happy together."

He did not look at her as he spoke.

Josina felt that he was thinking about what a catastrophe it was for him to have to marry a girl he had only seen for two days.

Also someone who had the stigma, as far as his family was concerned, of being the daughter of a gambler.

"So now you know," the Duke said briskly, "why I brought you here in such a hurry and I suggest that the most sensible thing for you to do would be to rest until I return, I hope, in only an hour or so with our Marriage Licence."

He paused and then continued,

"Of course no one in the house must know what is happening and certainly no one outside it."

"Your friends will – think it – very strange," Josina pointed out hesitantly.

"Naturally," the Duke agreed, "but I think, if you consider it carefully, my story would be difficult to disprove. After all your mother was not very old when she died and there would be no reason for me to believe that she would die when I left you looking after her in Italy."

Josina could not answer this.

He then walked across the room to his desk to pick up some papers.

"I will be as quick as I can," he said, "but it is possible that the formalities will take longer than one expects."

He moved towards the door and, as he reached it, he said,

"Just rest and don't worry. Things are never as bad as they seem."

Before Josina could say anything in reply he had gone.

She did not move for a little while, thinking that everything that was happening seemed like a bad dream that she could not awaken from.

How was it possible that the Duke of Nevondale, of all people, should marry her simply because she had helped him in such an unusual way?

'When he thinks about what has happened, he will hate me!' she told herself.

She wanted to run after him and tell him that whatever happened to her she would not marry him.

Then she knew that by this time he would be in the hall and there would be servants who would hear what they said.

'What can I do? *What can I do?*' she asked herself frantically.

She walked to the window and gazed out, seeing that there was a garden at the back of the house.

There were flowerbeds brilliant in the sunshine and two tall trees, which reminded her of The Hall.

How could she imagine that, after she had followed her mother's instructions to go to the Head of the Family for help, he would be forced into making her his wife?

'*Forced*' was the right word, Josina thought.

Of course he was being forced.

She was sure that the Comtesse had been right when she said that gentlemen avoided young girls and had as little to do with them as possible.

And she was quite certain that the last thing the Duke wanted was to be saddled with a wife, especially when he was in love with a sophisticated, clever, seductive woman like the *Comtesse.*

She felt again the sudden shock that she had experienced when she saw them in bed together.

It was then she knew that she could not marry the Duke.

Anything, anything would be better than being his wife, knowing that he did not want her and that they did not love each other.

But then, as she thought of him, she had the strange feeling that it would not be difficult for her to love anyone so handsome, so intelligent and so respected.

He was such a marvellous rider and she remembered how, when she had first seen him on a horse, she had felt a little thrill in her breast because he rode so well.

He looked completely magnificent on the huge stallion he was riding.

She had the same feeling when he came galloping towards the Winning Post at the Steeplechase.

She had held her breath and prayed that he would win.

For one agonising moment she had thought that Harry was in the lead and then by sheer expertise the Duke had seemed almost to lift his horse forward.

She could feel what she thought was her excitement pulsating again in her heart.

And yet she knew now that it was something stronger.

Something that, because she had never felt it before, she could not give it a name.

Now a voice seemed to be whispering to her that this was the beginning of love.

It was then that she threw out her hands as if to protect herself.

'No – no – *no!*'

She said the three words beneath her breath, yet they came from the very depths of her being.

How could she fall in love as her mother had done with her father and marry a man who did not love her?

She imagined that yearning for him as her mother had when her father had been away would be a living Hell.

When the Duke came back, he would look at her with indifference and wishing that she were someone else.

"I – cannot do it – *I cannot*!" she cried out aloud and thought that she would rather die.

It was then she knew that she must ask for help and the only help available was from God.

The Duke had said that they would be married at the Grosvenor Chapel and he had mentioned that it was not far from Nevon House.

As she thought about it, Josina remembered what she had heard about the Chapel.

When her mother had described Nevon House in Park Lane, she told her that she had always gone to Church on Sundays at the Grosvenor Chapel.

'Today is Sunday,' Josina reminded herself.

Because so much had happened, she had not thought until now that she should have gone to Church. It was something that she and her mother had always done wherever they were in the world.

Although most of the Churches they attended abroad were Roman Catholic, her mother told her that God would always hear their prayers in any Church.

Slowly Josina went from the study and up the stairs to her bedroom.

She knew when she saw her luggage being unpacked that Nanny had arrived.

As if she had asked the question, one of the housemaids who was putting her gowns into the wardrobe volunteered,

"Miss Tate's havin' somethin' to eat, miss, and His Grace ordered some food for you to be put in the boudoir."

"Thank you very much," Josina replied.

She walked across the room to what she was sure was the communicating door and then found herself in a very pretty boudoir.

There was a table already laid in front of the fireplace and to her relief there was no one to wait on her.

She thought perhaps the Duke had arranged this because he felt that she might be embarrassed.

She was not hungry, but she forced herself to eat a little of the salmon mousse that had been prepared in a silver dish.

She then drank a small amount of the white wine before going back into the bedroom.

She saw that the maids, having finished her unpacking, had gone.

Josina picked up the widow's bonnet that she had travelled in and, putting it on, pulled the veil down over her face.

Then she went downstairs and found that there two footmen on duty in the hall.

She thought they looked at her in surprise as she reached the front door.

"If anyone asks for me," she said, "I am just going to the Grosvenor Chapel. I know it is not very far from here."

"If you turns left, miss," one of the footmen answered, "then take the second turnin' left, you'll see it just ahead."

"Thank you."

"It won't take long, ma'am," the other footman suggested, "to fetch a carriage from the stables, if you'd wait for a moment or two."

"No thank you, I shall enjoy the walk in the fresh air," Josina replied.

He opened the front door for her.

And then following their directions she walked down a quiet street.

The first turning was into a Mews and the second one was just a slightly busier street.

But she could see what she was sure was the Grosvenor Chapel on the right hand side of the road.

She was remembering how her mother had said that, when she was a girl, the Grosvenor family always sat in a front pew on one side of the gallery.

The Nevons had sat on the other.

'I am sure if I pray to Mama where she prayed when she was my age, she will help me,' Josina told herself.

The door of the Chapel was open.

She went in and climbed up the steps to the gallery and she hoped that she had chosen the correct side as she sank down on her knees.

It was then that she prayed fervently and desperately for help,

'What am I to do, Mama?' she cried in her heart. 'You sent me to England to ask the Duke to look after me. How can I marry him when he – loves somebody – else? I always thought I would – marry a man – I loved – as you loved Papa. If I run away – as I want to do I have – no money.'

She felt that somehow she would hear her mother answer her.

Instead there was only silence.

Despairingly she looked at the altar, which was massed with white flowers.

Quite unexpectedly she heard the organ begin to be played very softly.

She had no idea that there was anybody else in the Chapel.

Yet now the music seemed to come like a message, not from the organ but from Heaven.

She felt her whole being respond to it, as if her mother was telling her not to be afraid.

She went on praying and now it was more like conversation as she told her mother how frightened she was.

Then, just as when she was a small child, her mother seemed to be holding her close and she was telling her that whatever happened she was never alone.

Because she was so deep in her thoughts Josina was not certain when the music stopped.

But she thought now that she must go back and she rose from her knees.

As she did so, she was aware that in some strange way she felt very different from when she had come into the Chapel.

She walked outside into the bright sunshine.

As she did so, she suddenly remembered what she had completely forgotten until now, that behind the Grosvenor Chapel there was a burial ground.

It was here, her mother had told her, that some of the members of her family had been laid to rest.

The burial ground had been allotted a century earlier to those who lived in the Parish of St. George's, Hanover Square.

When South Audley Street was built, Sir Richard Grosvenor had leased a plot of land for thirty pounds a year on which the Grosvenor Chapel had been built.

Behind it was the burial ground known as St. George's and tombs of both the Grosvenors and the Nevons were to be found there.

Josina thought that she would like to see if she could find her grandmother's grave.

She could see, just as her mother had told her, that quite a number of Nevons had very impressive tombstones.

Some graves had wreaths of flowers on them, but there were none on those of her relations.

It took some time for Josina to find her grandfather's large and important-looking tombstone,

As she looked at it, she saw that beside it was a very much smaller grave.

She then bent down to read what was carved on the stone.

"*LORD DUDLEY NEVON DIED 1789, AGED SIX.*"

And just below it she thought was inscribed,

"SUFFER THE LITTLE CHILDREN TO COME UNTO ME."

Pushing back her veil so that she could see a little better, Josina moved some moss from over the quotation.

Even as she did so, she was startled by a voice behind her saying,

"Excuse me, ma'am, but may I tell you that I have never seen anyone more beautiful than you look at this very moment!"

Josina looked up in astonishment and then saw standing above her there was an elderly man.

He was a very striking figure with a swarthy complexion and a white beard.

He looked, she reckoned, rather like a Prophet from the Old Testament of the Bible.

She had the impression, however, that his eyes were piercing and looking not at her face but deep down into her soul.

She raised herself up and realised that, as he was so tall, she only came up to his shoulder.

Because she felt a little embarrassed, she stammered,

"I-I was looking at the – tombstones."

"And making such a wonderful picture," the old man said, "that I am begging you, if necessary on my bended knees, to let me paint you."

Josina looked surprised and he explained,

"My name is Raphael Owen and, while I am not a very well-known artist, I am a friend and follower of George Watts, who I am sure you must have heard of."

"Yes, of course, I have heard of him," Josina replied. "He has painted some very fine pictures."

She was thinking of how her mother and she had studied the English artists who were best known.

Naturally George Frederick Watts was amongst them as well as Sir John Everett Millais, whose picture, *The Boyhood of Raleigh*, had been acclaimed all over the Continent.

"Let me explain, ma'am," Mr. Raphael Owen was saying, "how much I need you. The entries for the Royal Academy have to be in position in four days' time. I have tried, and only God knows how much I have tried, to find the inspiration which would portray something that every onlooker will understand and which at the same time has a message that will go to their hearts."

He spoke fervently as if every word was deeply sincere and Josina sensed that he was telling her the absolute truth.

He certainly looked like an artist.

He wore a velvet coat over his dark trousers and, instead of a collar and tie, he had a handkerchief tied round his neck that ended in a large bow.

"It seems like a miracle when I was in despair that at the very last moment I should find you and know that you are exactly what I want. Who could look at you in your widow's weeds, kneeling at the grave of a little boy and not be moved to tears?"

Because it mattered so much to him, Josina found herself saying,

"I would – like to help you, sir, but – I am afraid it is – impossible."

"But why, why?"

"Because I have just come to London – " she started to explain.

Then her voice stopped.

It flashed through her mind that perhaps the miracle she had been praying so hard for had happened.

Yet how could it possibly be true?

"You have come to London – ?" Mr. Raphael Owen prompted. "You are here and I am here and how can anything prevent me from painting anyone so exquisitely lovely?"

"The difficulty is, sir," Josina said, feeling as if the words were being put into her mouth, "that I have – nowhere to – go."

"Nowhere to go?"

There was no doubt that her answer surprised the artist.

"I am – alone," Josina told him, "and this is the – first time that I have been – in London."

"Then, of course, I must ask you if you will honour my poor house by staying with me," Mr. Raphael Owen said. "My housekeeper, a very worthy woman, will look after you and do her best to make you comfortable. If you will only stay for three days, I can paint you as I see you now and you will make an old man very happy."

Josina drew in her breath.

Could this really be happening? How could she accept his invitation?

The Duke would be waiting for her with the Marriage Licence.

If she was not there, there would be nothing he could do.

And at least she would have time to think and perhaps find some way by which she could support herself.

The artist was watching her, aware of the indecision in her eyes.

Equally he could see that she was considering what he had suggested.

"How can I beg of you to help me and make you realise how grateful I should be for your kindness? I can assure you that you will be safe and not asked to do anything that you do not wish to do."

He paused and then continued,

"Indeed as I have already said, my housekeeper will look after you and you will be treated with the utmost respect by her *and by me.*"

He accentuated the last words as if he felt that Josina was thinking that he might in some way impose himself on her as a man.

He was well aware that artists had a reputation for immorality and for their pursuit of women.

He could understand how this exquisite creature, who seemed to him to have come from another planet, was worried.

She was afraid of being in a dangerous situation that she could not extract herself from easily.

Feeling sure that this was what she was thinking, he went on,

"I am an old man, in fact over seventy and, while I worship beauty wherever I find it, it is no longer within my grasp."

He realised as he spoke that Josina did not understand what he meant.

He therefore merely added,

"I beg of you, madam, if you care for art, as I am sure you do, to help me create a picture which I will be proud to hang in the Royal Academy. And we are wasting time standing about talking when we might be getting down to work!"

Because his last words were a change from the way he had spoken before, Josina laughed.

"It is difficult to know how to refuse you, sir," she said, "but I must explain before I come to you – that I have no money and nothing – but what I stand up in."

"Why should you want money when I will pay you?" Mr. Raphael Owen enquired. "In fact I will pay you anything you ask if you will 'sit' for me, as the expression goes."

"You will – pay – me?" Josina asked.

She had not realised that artists' models were paid for their services.

"Of course I will pay you," Mr. Raphael Owen replied, "at least four or five pounds more than any other model can command at this moment from my contemporaries."

Josina then made up her mind.

"I-I will be pleased to – come with you, sir."

The artist threw up his hands and glanced up at the sky saying as he did so,

"Thank you, *thank you*! You have saved me as you have saved me before, but this has been at the very last moment!"

If he had prayed for help, Josina thought, it was what she too had prayed for.

In a strange and most unusual way her prayers had been answered and she was quite certain now that it was her mother who had guided her to the right place at the right moment.

Now she would not have to marry the Duke and be desperately unhappy at having to do so.

She wanted to run back into the Grosvenor Chapel and thank both her mother and God for helping her.

Then she thought that she need not go back to the Chapel, she could thank them here from where she was standing.

She smiled at the artist.

Then she went down on her knees beside the grave of the small boy and touched the stone with her fingers.

'Thank you, thank you, Mama,' she said in her heart, 'and I thank too the little boy who, as one of my relations, has helped me.'

She promised herself that, as soon as she had some money of her own, she would come back and place some flowers on the small grave.

She rose to her feet and said to the artist who was watching her,

"Now, sir, perhaps you will show me where we have to go."

"It's not far from here," he said. "I live in a house in Farm Street."

They walked across the graveyard and out through a different entrance from the one that Josina had come through earlier.

As she went, she was thinking how horrified her Nevon relations would be if they knew what she was doing.

She thought that it would be what they would expect of the daughter of a gambler.

She was in fact gambling in what anyone would consider was a very reckless and reprehensible way.

She was entrusting herself to a strange man she had never seen until a few minutes ago and she was going with him to his house without any luggage and without any money.

Just for a moment she felt afraid.

Then she knew that, if it was not what she expected and if Mr. Raphael Owen was not what he professed to be, she could return to Nevon House.

She could ask the Duke to forgive her.

'He will undoubtedly be very angry that I should disappear without any explanation,' she reflected.

At the same time she was quite sure that he would be relieved at not having to marry a girl he had known only since the day before yesterday.

He would not be encumbered with a tiresome *debutante* nor would he have to worry as to what his relatives would think of her.

Doubtless, as he was so clever, he would think of a reasonable explanation as to why she had disappeared.

If the story of the Comte was repeated, he would merely say that the lady who had occupied his bed was someone he had met on the Continent and she had followed him back to England.

'And that,' Josina said to herself as she walked with Mr. Raphael Owen into Farm Street, 'will be the end of the story.'

CHAPTER SEVEN

Mr. Owen's house was very old and squeezed between two very much larger ones.

As he took Josina through the front door, she was suddenly aware that, although she was dressed as a widow, she was not wearing a Wedding ring.

With a sense of relief she remembered that she had changed the trimming on her bonnet in the waiting room when she arrived and had slipped off the Wedding ring.

It was therefore still in her handbag where she had put it.

She was ready when a minute later Mr. Owen suggested,

"You must tell me your name, beautiful lady."

"I am Mrs. Musgrove," Josina replied. "Josie Musgrove."

She thought as she spoke that these were names that she would be able to remember.

By this time they were in a small hall with a wooden staircase rising on one side of it.

Mr. Owen then shouted out,

"I am back! *I am back!*"

An elderly woman came then through the door at the end of the passage and said,

"I was wonderin' what had 'appened to you."

"I have won! *I have won!*" Mr. Owen exclaimed in excited tones. "I have found what I was seeking and you, Mrs. Finch, must look after her."

Looking not in the least surprised, as if this had happened many times before, Mrs. Finch came forward.

Mr. Owen introduced them proudly and added,

"It was like a light in the darkness when I saw her bending over the grave. I know now that I have my picture and it will prove to be a great success."

"Well, you'll certainly have to 'urry up about it," Mrs. Finch said practically. "You've only got three days."

"I know," Mr. Owen answered. "I am going to ask you, Mrs. Musgrove, to come upstairs with me now."

He turned towards the staircase and Josina said, feeling slightly embarrassed, to Mrs. Finch,

"Mr. Owen has not explained to you – but I-I have only just arrived in London and I have – no luggage with me, but he has been kind enough to tell me that I can – stay here."

For a moment Mrs. Finch looked surprised, then as if she was used to any emergency, whatever it might be, she said,

"Don't you worry, my dear, we'll cope some'ow. As long as he's got the inspiration 'e needs that's all that matters. He's bin drivin' me nearly mad these last few weeks!"

Without saying anything more she disappeared the way she had come.

Josina followed Mr. Owen up the stairs and found after two flights that he had made what had once been the attics of the house into a studio.

The ceiling was beamed and arched and at the same time he had built in a large North window.

She knew that this was what every serious artist required.

All around the walls canvasses were stacked and she could see that he had started to paint on some of them, but had given up before the pictures were finished.

Mr. Owen was in the process of moving a chair from the dais that was in the centre of the room.

He placed a plain canvas against a stool and she knew that it was intended to be the gravestone.

"Now," he said in an excited voice, "bend down, or better still, kneel as you were when I first saw you."

Josina obeyed him, pushing back her veil as she did so.

"Put out your hand," Mr. Owen next asked her.

She remembered that this was how she had removed the moss from the inscription beneath the little boy's name.

Mr. Owen looked at her first one way and then the other.

Finally, he found the position he wanted and with a cry of excitement adjusted his easel.

Then he squeezed some colour from a tube and started to paint what he saw in front of him.

*

The next day Josina was thinking by the time the afternoon came that she had never found anything more difficult or more tiring.

Mr. Owen grew angry if she moved and she found her knees and her back beginning to ache until it was agony.

They had a very quick luncheon and then went back once again and she took up her pose.

The only way that she could forget how uncomfortable she felt was when she thought about the Duke.

Last night, when she had gone to bed in the small narrow room, which she gathered was the only spare bedroom in the house, she had cried herself to sleep.

It was one thing to know that she had done what was right and had saved the Duke from being forced into a marriage he did not want.

It was quite another to know how unhappy she would be without him and how her heart tried to persuade her to return to him.

'If you were married to him,' voices tempted her, 'you would at least be able to see him every day. You would hear his voice and he would be kind to you because he is a very kind man.'

It would not be what she wanted, but it would certainly be better than being alone in the world. And better than being in a country where she had no friends and only hostile relatives who she could not approach.

Yet she knew that if she was to marry the Duke it would be worse than the agony of being alone and unprotected.

He would never love her as she loved him.

'And I do – love him, Mama, *I do*!' she sobbed into her pillow. 'Why could I not have met someone who would – love me as Papa – loved you?'

She thought how wonderful it was that her father and mother had fallen in love at first sight.

Whatever the difficulties, they had known that they could not lose each other.

'That is what I – wanted and what I – prayed for,' Josina said bitterly in her heart.

*

When morning came and she awoke, Mrs. Finch told her that breakfast would be ready in half-an-hour.

When she looked in the mirror she saw that her face was very pale and there were dark shadows under her eyes.

Mr. Owen, however, did not seem to notice.

She was back in the same position by nine o'clock.

He worked without stopping until Mrs. Finch told them that luncheon was ready.

It was late in the afternoon when Josina thought that she must ask Mr. Owen to let her rest.

Then the door of the attic opened and a man's voice called out,

"I knew where I would find you, Owen, so I told your housekeeper that there was no need to announce me."

Mr. Owen looked up from his easel.

With a little sigh of relief Josina dropped her arm and straightened her back.

"I was not expecting you, Sir Eustace," Mr. Owen greeted the newcomer, "and, as you can see, I am very busy."

"Not too busy for me," Sir Eustace answered, walking down the room towards him. "I have a commission for you that I think you will appreciate."

"That is very kind of you," Mr. Owen replied, "but I must have this finished for the Royal Academy and I have never been more certain in my life that it will be a huge popular success."

For the first time Sir Eustace looked at Josina and there was an expression of surprise on his face.

He was a man of about forty, tall, good-looking and with broad shoulders.

However Josina felt that there was something about him that she did not like.

She could not put it into words, but the feeling was definitely strong.

"Now I see what you are painting, Owen," Sir Eustace said slowly, "I am prepared to believe you."

He walked towards Josina asking,

"Who is this lovely creature and why have I not seen her before?"

"We met in the graveyard," Mr. Owen replied, "and I knew when I saw her looking at the grave of a small boy that the picture I would paint of her would bring tears to the eyes of everyone who saw it."

"It does not bring tears to my eyes," Sir Eustace said, "but admiration for anyone so exquisite and so lovely."

He put out his hand towards Josina as he demanded,

"Tell me your name unless it is 'Aphrodite' and you have come from Mount Olympus to bemuse we poor mortals!"

Josina, who had been crouching down, now rose to her feet.

She put her hand into Sir Eustace's and as she did so she became aware that her feeling that there was something unpleasant about him was absolutely right.

His fingers closed over hers.

She knew that what he was feeling about her was something that she did not want and should try at all costs to avoid.

As she did not speak, Mr. Owen said,

"My model is called 'Mrs. Musgrove' and now please, Sir Eustace, let me get on with my work."

"I am delighted for you to be able to do so," Sir Eustace replied, "but I will want you, or rather your model, to tell me what I am waiting to hear, if she has just come from Mount Olympus."

He seated himself as he spoke in an armchair near the dais.

Knowing what was expected, Josina crouched down again as she had been doing before.

She was, however, instantly aware of Sir Eustace's eyes looking at her in a way that she found embarrassing.

There was also something insulting in the way that he was eyeing her.

She had the feeling that he was mentally undressing her and that his interest in her was definitely dangerous.

It was a relief when Mrs. Finch came to the door to say,

"Your tea's ready, Master, and I'm not carryin' it up all them stairs for three of those as has use of their legs!"

She did not wait for Mr. Owen to reply, but went downstairs again.

Sir Eustace rose to his feet.

"I would enjoy a cup of tea," he said, "and it will give me a chance to talk to this beautiful lady and learn what you are both reluctant to tell me."

There was nothing that Josina could do but go downstairs with the two men.

She did, however, stop at the first floor with the excuse that she wanted to wash her hands.

In her bedroom she tidied her hair under her bonnet with its black veil.

She was wishing that she could pull the veil over her face so that Sir Eustace could not see her.

He tried to talk to her at tea and she answered him in monosyllables.

It was a relief when the meal was ended and Josina knew then that Mr. Owen would go back to the studio to carry on with the painting and Sir Eustace would have to leave.

As he said 'goodbye', he held Josina's hand in both of his and expounded,

"We shall meet again, my beautiful little Aphrodite, make no mistake about that. I can understand our host's desire to put you on canvas, but I have very different ideas, which I will tell you about later."

Josina did not answer him.

She had some difficulty in taking her hand away from his and she then hurried up the stairs and Mr. Owen followed her.

She knew without looking back that Sir Eustace was watching her go and only when she was back on the dais in the studio did she feel safe from him.

At the same time she had learnt over tea that he had a very important and influential friend, the Lord Lieutenant of Huntingdonshire.

He had suggested to him that Raphael Owen would paint a better and a cheaper portrait them anybody else.

"Thank you," Mr. Owen had said to him. "I am indeed grateful to you, Sir Eustace, and of course, as soon as my present job is finished, I will be in touch with Lord Lansdown."

"I just cannot imagine you will ever finish the job of painting Aphrodite," Sir Eustace responded looking at Josina.

Mr. Owen did not answer.

Now he picked up his paintbrush and as he did so he commented,

"Sir Eustace is noted as being a 'lady killer'. But he is very rich and you could do worse."

Josina did not know exactly what he meant, but she replied quickly,

"I-I don't – want to see him again – and I hope that – tomorrow he will not – disturb us."

"I hope so too," Mr. Owen declared. "If there is one thing I dislike, it's people talking to me and looking over my shoulder as I paint!

He spoke crossly, but Josina was aware that Sir Eustace was far too important a man for him to either insult or ignore.

To her relief he did not appear the next day.

The day after that, by what seemed to be a superhuman effort, Mr. Owen had practically finished the picture.

But Josina felt again as if her back was breaking.

When she finally looked at the picture, she thought that it was extremely clever and beautifully done in the way that her mother had explained to her that Watts painted.

Mr. Owen's picture was not just a portrait.

It had an imaginary power about it that changed it into something quite different.

It also had the gentle allure of Watts's colour harmonies, which made her seem not exactly real but part of a dream.

She had glanced at the other pictures that were in the studio and she was aware that, like Watts, he added his allegories and fantasies to reality.

In fact she thought that it was rather hard to recognise herself because he had made her so ethereal that she seemed like a spirit from another planet.

Mr. Owen had gone out early in the morning to copy the tombstone of the little Lord Dudley Nevon exactly.

It was only when she had seen it that Josina had said,

"I think, if you will forgive me saying so, that it is a mistake to put the real name on the tombstone."

"Why should you say that?" Mr. Owen asked. "After all the boy died nearly a century ago."

Josina did not answer and he looked at her before he promised,

"But, of course, if it disturbs you personally, I will change it."

Josina clasped her hands together.

"Please," she insisted, "please do so. It cannot – matter to you, but it might matter – very much – to me."

Mr. Owen gave her a piercing glance and she had the idea that he was too tactful and too kind to press her for an explanation.

Instead he said,

"I will change the name, if you insist. Will that please you?"

Josina smiled.

"Thank you – thank you very much. That will be very kind."

Mr. Owen did as she asked him and she hoped and prayed that no one would connect the picture with the Nevon family.

She could not imagine that the Duke, with all his magnificent pictures, would visit the Royal Academy.

Yet even to think of him doing so gave her a little throb of pain in her breast.

At last the picture was finished even to Raphael Owen's satisfaction.

He went off with it to the Royal Academy with both Mrs. Finch and Josina wishing him luck.

"There's no question," Mrs. Finch explained as he drove away, "of them not 'angin' anythin' he paints, but all the artists struggle for the best position and that's, of course, what the Master wants."

"I hope he gets it," Josina sighed. "He is so very kind to me in letting me stay here with you and I am deeply grateful."

"I likes 'avin' you 'ere and that's the truth," Mrs. Finch said. "You're not like a model, nasty pieces of work some of 'em are, findin' fault and flirtin' with every man as comes through the door."

She sounded so disapproving that Josina could do nothing but laugh.

"I promise you I will not behave like that and do please let me help you."

"I'll tell you what you can do," Mrs. Finch answered, "Not today, because you're tired, but tomorrow. If you'll tidy up the studio for me, I'll be real grateful. The Master gets annoyed if I moves anythin' and a nice mess it's in. But 'e won't feel the same about you doin' it."

"Of course I will do it," Josina replied.

Mr. Owen came back later delighted.

Everybody at the Royal Academy had praised his picture and tomorrow when they were hung it would go in one of the very best places.

There would be a special opening when only the most influential people would be admitted and then they would let in the public.

"I will take you to see it the day after tomorrow," he promised. "You will be able to admire yourself and watch dozens of other people doing the same."

Josina smiled.

She had the feeling that it would be a mistake for her to be seen at the Royal Academy, but she did not say so at this moment.

Instead, as they sat down to supper, Mr. Owen started to talk about another picture that he wanted to paint of her.

"Sir Eustace called you 'Aphrodite'," he said, "and I would like to paint you as the Goddess and perhaps make it a more imaginary picture than I have ever done before. I could have her moving, as if it was through space with planets, suns and stars surrounding her."

"It sounds a wonderful idea," Josina enthused.

She thought that it would make a striking picture and it meant that Mr. Owen would want her to sit for it.

She had been so afraid that now his picture for the Royal Academy was finished he would suggest that she left.

She had nowhere to go.

As he had not yet mentioned what he was paying her, she had no money except for a few pounds in her handbag.

'I am safe here,' she thought that night.

While her heart cried out for the Duke, she did not cry.

She only lay thinking that her mother was looking after her and the future was not so frightening as it had seemed a few days ago.

*

The following day after a light luncheon, Raphael Owen dressed in his best and with his shoes highly polished by Mrs. Finch left for the Royal Academy.

Josina then went upstairs.

She had already started tidying some of the many canvasses that lay scattered around the studio.

There were empty tubes of oil paints that should have been thrown away a long time ago and there were dirty brushes in a jar of something that had once been used to clean them.

On a desk there were a number of sketches that Mr. Owen had made on the backs of envelopes and pieces of paper.

Occasionally they were on smart writing paper bearing a coronet or a crest over the address.

Josina guessed that this must have been when he was staying with someone important whose portrait he had been painting.

She was sure that the one he was to paint of the Lord Lieutenant of Huntingdonshire would be sensational and she hoped that it would bring him many more commissions.

The afternoon wore on with the studio beginning to look more and more tidy and much cleaner than when she had arrived.

Then the door opened and she thought that Mr. Owen had returned.

"Have you had – ?" she began and then stopped.

It was not Raphael Owen who came into the studio but Sir Eustace.

He walked towards her and she felt as if his eyes were devouring her as he did so.

"I have come to tell you, my beautiful Aphrodite, that your picture has been a huge success. There were crowds around it and I heard people saying more complimentary things about it than any other picture on the walls."

"Oh, I am glad – very glad!" Josina cried.

"And now," Sir Eustace went on, "you and I can talk about ourselves or rather I can talk about you, as Raphael has prevented me from doing these past days."

"There is – really nothing to – say," Josina remarked quickly.

Sir Eustace smiled.

"On the contrary, *I* have a great deal to say."

He walked towards the window of the studio and looked out.

"With your looks," he said, "you can hardly want to stay here, unseen and unknown."

"That is what I am – quite happy – to do."

"Nonsense!" Sir Eustace replied. "I am prepared to offer you a very comfortable house in Chelsea, a carriage of your own and, of course, the most beautiful gowns that Bond Street can supply."

Josina stared at him as if she thought that she could not have heard right.

Then slowly and incredulously she was aware of what he was implying.

The colour drained from her face as she said in a voice that did not sound like her own,

"I think, sir, you are being – extremely insulting!"

"Stop playing hard to get," Sir Eustace replied. "No woman is insulted at being offered a frame for her beauty and diamonds that glitter as brightly as her eyes."

Josina lifted her chin.

"Then I must be the exception, for my answer is quite clear. I am perfectly content to stay as I am. I want nothing – nothing that – you could offer me."

Sir Eustace smiled.

"Then I must take what I want, my lovely one and I assure you that I am never defeated in the first skirmish."

He reached out his arm as he spoke.

Because Josina was not expecting it, he swept her close to his chest and held her tightly against him.

For a moment she was surprised into immobility.

Then, as she realised that he was about to kiss her, she tried to push him away from her.

He was a very large man and she recognised with a sense of panic that she was completely imprisoned in his arms!

The supreme effort that she was making to free herself was completely ineffectual.

His head came down and she turned her face from side to side in an attempt to avoid his lips.

She became aware that in some strange manner her opposition excited him and made him more determined than ever to conquer her.

Finally, holding her with one arm in a grip of steel, with the other he took possession of her chin and turned her face up to his.

For a moment he looked down at her.

She saw the fire in his eyes and the smile of satisfaction on his lips.

She was helpless, utterly helpless in his grasp, and he knew it.

She gave a scream and then another and as she did so the door of the studio opened.

Josina heard it.

With a superhuman effort she managed in a split second to turn her face to one side so that Sir Eustace's lips only touched her cheek.

As she screamed again, a voice asked harshly,

"What the devil is going on here?"

As the visitor spoke, Josina stiffened thinking that it could not be true.

It was not Mr. Owen who had come into the studio, but *the Duke*!

The sound of his voice and the knowledge that he was walking towards them made Sir Eustace slacken his hold.

Josina fought herself free and ran towards the Duke.

She met him halfway across the studio and flung herself against him.

"Save me – oh – *save me*!" she cried and hid her face against his shoulder.

The Duke put his arms around her as if to prevent her from falling and stared at Sir Eustace.

"It would appear, Wake," he said grimly, "that you are up to your tricks again. I think it would be wise if you left now."

There was an expression of fury on Sir Eustace's face.

But he had too much respect for the Duke's position to put into words what he was feeling.

"I had no idea, Nevondale," he replied, "that you were interested in Owen's new model, but if that is the position then, of course, I will withdraw."

With that he walked towards the door of the studio, pulling his coat into place as he went.

As he disappeared from sight, the Duke's arms tightened round Josina and he said,

"How could you do anything so utterly and completely *damnable* as to run away and leave me desperate at not knowing what had happened to you?"

There was a pause before Josina managed to whisper,

"I-I had to – g-go."

"But, why?" the Duke asked.

"Because – I knew that – you did not – really want to – marry me and – ?"

"Why should you think that?" the Duke interrupted.

"You were – just being – kind in – saving my reputation – which does not – matter to anyone – and it was wrong for you to be – married in such a – foolish manner."

She had difficulty in making the Duke understand what she was saying, but he listened.

Then he said quietly,

"You might have discussed it with me first."

"You – you had – said it was what I – had to do and you were – being kind for m-my sake – but I am all right here – and if anyone asked what has – happened to me – you can say that I am – dead."

The Duke made a little sound that was half a laugh.

"Do you really think that is what I would do?" he asked. "Oh, my darling, how can you be so ridiculous?"

Josina could hardly believe what he had just said.

She was very still and the Duke went on,

"We have a great deal to explain to each other, but now I just want to look at you."

Gently he turned her face up to his and sighed,

"You are even more beautiful than your picture and much more beautiful than I remember."

"You – you have – s-seen my – picture?" Josina asked. "I-I did not – think you would – go to the – Royal Academy."

"I took my Godmother who wanted to see a portrait that had been painted of her," the Duke explained. "When I saw Owen's picture of you hanging on the wall, I knew that I had found you."

"You – you were – looking for – me?"

"Of course I was looking for you. I have searched London, I have had the Police alerted in case you had had an accident and your Nanny has been in tears ever since you left."

"And – and you really wanted to – f-find me?" Josina enquired.

She could hardly ask the question and yet it was said.

"That is what I have come to tell you," and now that I have found you, I swear that I will never lose you again."

"But – why? Why – when you can be – free?"

The Duke smiled.

"The truth is, my darling, that I do *not* want to be free. I love you and I think, although perhaps it is extraordinary, that you love me too."

Josina was sure that she was dreaming.

Because the Duke was looking at her and because of the soft note in his voice, she found herself saying,

"I do – love you! *I love you* – but I thought I would never – see you again.'"

As she spoke, her voice broke and tears came into her eyes and ran down her cheeks.

"My sweet, my darling," the Duke exclaimed. "That is what I wanted to hear. But how could you go away, if you loved me? How could you leave me? I have been almost crazy with worry thinking that I would never find you."

"I-I loved you – so much," Josina whispered, "that I thought it would be – agony to m-marry you – knowing you loved – somebody else."

She gave a little gasp as she said the words and tried to hide her face again.

The Duke prevented her from doing so and said,

"I think you are speaking of the Comtesse. How can I make you believe, my darling, that I fell in love with you from the first moment I saw you? I knew then that you are the woman I have been looking for all my life."

He gave a deep sigh as he added,

"When I knew how innocent and unspoiled you are, I was horrified to think that you were in the party that was taking place at that moment."

Josina looked bewildered.

"I-I did not understand – I thought you – loved – her."

She was thinking as she spoke of the shock it had been when she had gone into the Duke's bedroom and seen them together in bed.

To her surprise the Duke picked her up in his arms and carried her to a sofa that stood against one of the walls.

He sat down holding her across his knees as if she was a child.

"Now listen, my lovely one," he said. "I have something to tell you and I want you to believe me because we must start our lives together without there being any secrets between us."

Because of what he was saying, Josina felt a little thrill run through her.

Without actually meaning to, she moved a little nearer to him.

Then he said,

"I found the Comtesse very amusing and attractive until I saw you. When you came into the room, you seemed to be surrounded by an aura of light."

He paused and then continued,

"I realised then that you were different from the other women I knew and you were what I have been seeking in my heart."

"Is that – true – really true?" Josina asked.

"Do you think I would lie to you now at this particular moment?" the Duke asked. "You know it is true."

He saw the look of rapture that came into her face.

He knew that no one could be more beautiful or lovelier.

With an effort he went on,

"I swear to you on everything I hold holy that I never touched or made love to the Comtesse again after you arrived at The Hall."

He spoke slowly, as if he was making a vow and, seeing the question in Josina's eyes, he said,

"The first night you came I made the excuse that I needed to sleep because of the Steeplechase and the next night I locked my door."

There was a slight pause before he added,

"But like you, the Comtesse came to me through the boudoir."

Josina drew in her breath.

As she did so, she remembered that, when she reached the Duke's bedroom, she had heard the Comtesse talking to him in a cross and petulant voice.

"You know what happened then," the Duke went on. "You saved me, my darling, saved me from finding myself in a very uncomfortable position and being, I am sure, forced to fight a duel that I had no interest in winning."

"I-I was – afraid – desperately afraid – you might – d-die as my Papa died," Josina whispered.

"But I am alive and when we came to London I was thinking how wonderful it would be when we were married and I could tell you how much I love you."

"You – you never – said anything."

"I thought that you would not understand, seeing the position I had been in the previous night and that I would have plenty of time later when we were alone and you were my wife to tell you how deeply I love you and how I prayed that you would love me."

"*I do – love you*! I loved you, I think, from the moment – I first saw you, but I did not know at first that it was love," Josina replied, "and when I did – 1 thought – how unhappy and miserable I would be if – you did not – want my love."

She could hardly say the words and managed to turn her face against his chest again.

The Duke understood exactly what she was saying.

There was a tender expression in his eyes that no other woman had ever seen.

"My precious, my darling," he suggested, "let's go home now and we will be married as soon as I can find a Parson to make you my wife."

Josina looked up at him again.

"You are – quite certain – quite – quite certain," she said, "that you – really – want me?"

"So certain," the Duke insisted, "that I am not going to wait another minute. We are leaving now and we will come and tell Owen all about it tomorrow. But I cannot delay any longer in doing what is the most exciting thing that has ever happened to me in my whole life."

Because he sounded so elated, Josina gave a little cry of joy.

Then hand-in-hand, they ran towards the door.

*

Later that night Josina moved her head against her husband's shoulder and whispered,

"I-I have – something to – ask you."

"What is it, my precious?" the Duke enquired.

"You do not – find me – boring after all – the exciting and – sophisticated – women you have – known?"

He knew exactly what she was asking and that this was a very important question.

He answered her gently,

"Let me tell you, my lovely adorable little wife, that never, and this is the truth, never have I known such ecstasy, such rapture, as when I made you mine."

"Is that – can that – really be – possible?" Josina asked. "I felt as if you – carried me up into the sky – but I was so – afraid that I was not – doing exactly what – you wanted."

The Duke gave a laugh that was very tender.

"No one could be more wonderful or more exactly what I prayed for and hoped someday I would find."

His arms tightened as he said,

"You are mine – mine, my darling – mine from the top of your golden head to your tiny feet and I worship you, as I shall do for the rest of my life."

Josina gave a little gasp before she murmured,

"That makes – me very happy. I was so – afraid that I would – fail you – as Mama never – failed Papa."

"You are perfect, completely and absolutely perfect. We are going to be very happy together, my beautiful wife, just as your mother and father were. And we will make everybody around us as happy as we are."

"That is – what I would – like to – do," Josina agreed, "but because you are – very important – I am afraid people will think it – strange that you should have – married me, especially our – Nevon relations."

"When they see you, no one will be surprised that I married you," the Duke said, "because you are so beautiful, but I can promise you one thing, even if our relations do disapprove of you and me, they will be far too frightened to say so."

He gave a short laugh.

"But we shall never know what they do think because I promise you they will keep it to themselves."

"Can that – really – be true?"

"You will learn as the years go by that I am speaking the truth and they will admire you as a very beautiful and very *important* Duchess."

He accentuated the word 'important' and Josina understood.

Of course, instead of being a poor Nevon relation, the daughter of a gambler, she would seem very different as the Duke's wife and chatelaine of all his houses.

She moved a little closer to him.

"It is a – Fairytale," she whispered, "and you are the – Prince Charming who came to – rescue me when I least – expected it. I am so very very lucky and I shall thank God – again and again that I – found you."

"As I have found you, my darling, and I will never lose you. You are mine, mine for ever."

His lips were seeking hers and his hand moved over her body.

Then he was one with her, passionately, possessively and completely.

She knew that he was carrying her again up into the sky where they were touching the peaks of ecstasy.

They moved into a Heaven that she had always known existed, but thought that she would never find.

It was the Heaven of *real* Love, which God keeps for lovers.

OTHER BOOKS IN THIS SERIES

The Barbara Cartland Eternal Collection is the unique opportunity to collect all five hundred of the timeless beautiful romantic novels written by the world's most celebrated and enduring romantic author.

Named the Eternal Collection because Barbara's inspiring stories of pure love, just the same as love itself, the books will be published on the internet at the rate of four titles per month until all five hundred are available.

The Eternal Collection, classic pure romance available worldwide for all time.

www.ingramcontent.com/pod-product-compliance
Lightning Source LLC
Chambersburg PA
CBHW022112170626
46808CB00002B/706

* 9 7 8 1 7 8 8 6 7 1 5 0 7 *